'I'm so sorry about that,' Harry said as he took Phoebe in his arms on the dance floor. 'I'd forgotten just how much my aunt pries.'

'Don't be,' she said. 'She is only looking after your interests, protecting you from the husband-hunting part of the local community—clearly she thinks I might be one of them!'

'And are you?' he asked quizzically, with his good humour restored.

'That's for me to know and you to find out,' she said laughingly—and, with the heady excitement of being dressed up and out for the evening with the man she could so easily fall in love with making her heart beat faster, she gave herself up to the moment...

Dear Reader

Welcome to the first of my books where coast and countryside combine to bring you the beautiful Devon village of *Bluebell Cove*. A place where doctors and nurses in the medical practice look after the health of the local folk and share their joys and sorrows, and in return have the respect and support of their patients when it is their turn to need a friend.

I live in a village in the Cheshire countryside myself, and it never ceases to amaze me how close is the bond between those who live here. When one of them hurts they all hurt. When one of them rejoices they all rejoice.

In THE VILLAGE NURSES'S HAPPY-EVER-AFTER nurse Phoebe Howard comes to the sanctuary of Bluebell Cove to find a home for herself and her baby boy. Romance is not on her agenda until she meets her gorgeous new boss.

If you have enjoyed reading about the folks there, do look out for their stories in Book two, CHRISTMAS IN BLUEBELL COVE, also available this month. Book four will be coming along shortly.

So do let's keep in touch, dear reader, as I write and you read about golden beaches, clotted cream teas, and *romance* in Devon—glorious Devon!

Abigail Gordon

THE
VILLAGE NURSE'S
HAPPY-EVER AFTER

BY
ABIGAIL GORDON

MILLS
BOON

First published in Great Britain 2010
Harlequin Mills & Boon Limited,
Eton House, 18-24 Paradise Road, Richmond, Surrey TW9 1SR

© Abigail Gordon 2010

ISBN: 978 0 263 21520 5

Harlequin Mills & Boon policy is to use papers that are natural, renewable and recyclable products and made from wood grown in sustainable forests. The logging and manufacturing process conform to the legal environmental regulations of the country of origin.

Printed and bound in Great Britain
by CPI Antony Rowe, Chippenham, Wiltshire

Abigail Gordon loves to write about the fascinating combination of medicine and romance from her home in a Cheshire village. She is active in local affairs, and is even called upon to write the script for the annual village pantomime! Her eldest son is a hospital manager, and helps with all her medical research. As part of a close-knit family, she treasures having two of her sons living close by, and the third one not too far away. This also gives her the added pleasure of being able to watch her delightful grandchildren growing up.

Recent titles by the same author:

CHAPTER ONE

PHOEBE HOWARD had moved into the apartment above The Tides Medical Practice, in the coastal Devon village of Bluebell Cove, on the first day of January. She'd looked around it sombrely and thought it was adequate in a basic sort of way—it would have to do.

Looking down at the toddler in her arms, she'd said, 'It has one advantage, Marcus. Your mummy won't have to travel far to work as she's based right here. We have Ethan to thank for this—him, and your Aunt Katie and Uncle Rob, who took me in when I was a lost soul. They are the ones who've always been there for me and I will be forever grateful.

'But now Ethan has found the happiness he so much deserves, and is going to live in Paris with his lovely family. At the same time Katie and Rob are moving up north to be near his elderly father, so it's just you and me from now on, little one. Oh, and with a new head of the practice to get used to thrown in for good measure!'

That had been a couple of weeks ago and today Phoebe was at the airport, along with other folk from Bluebell Cove, to say goodbye to the Lomax family as they departed for their new life in France.

In her role as district nurse at the village surgery, she'd arranged her home visits to her patients to leave her free for this moment. Once she'd seen the aircraft take off, it would be time to pick Marcus up from the Tiny Toes Nursery where he was being cared for while she was working.

It had been a wrench, taking him there. They'd spent barely any time apart since the day of his birth. During the months of her maternity leave, she'd lived with her sister Katie and brother-in-law Rob in the bustling market town near Bluebell Cove. On the rare occasions when she'd left Marcus, they had cared for him as lovingly as she did herself, but all the time she'd known it couldn't last. And even though she'd accepted that she had no choice, she still hated leaving him behind every day.

She knew she was fortunate, however, to have such a job. Her sister had seen the vacancy for district nurse in the nearby village of Bluebell Cove advertised on an NHS website. It had become reality from the moment that Ethan Lomax, the likeable head of the practice, had offered her the position. She'd worked there for the last few months of her pregnancy, until she'd started her maternity leave, staying with Katie and Rob.

But as they were moving up north to be near Rob's father it had meant that she'd had to find somewhere else to live. When Ethan had suggested she rent one of the two apartments above the surgery at a nominal rate, she'd been only too eager to accept.

After the noise and bustle of London—and the hurt she'd received there, she was as happy as circumstances permitted in Bluebell Cove. It had seemed strange when she'd first moved there, but it hadn't taken long for the peace and beauty of the place to charm her. She'd soon begun to feel a degree of contentment that she could never have expected so soon in her disrupted life. Now she no longer wept endlessly for what might have been. She was taking control of her life again as best she could, and if she had to hand Marcus over to others to be looked after while she was working, then that was how it would have to be.

As Phoebe watched, the Lomax family waved their last goodbyes and disappeared from sight. Soon the aircraft would be lifting off the runway, leaving yet another vacuum in her life. Suddenly holding back tears, Phoebe went to find her little car and drove off into the cold January afternoon.

At the end of the long flight from Australia, Harry Balfour gazed down sombrely on to the patchwork of towns, motorways and countryside that came into view as the pilot began the descent from the sky.

He was returning to the place of his birth, seeking solace and hoping to find it among the rolling green fields and magical coastline of Devon. It was where he'd always belonged, until five years ago when he'd met a feisty Australian girl. After a whirlwind romance, he'd married her and gone to live in her country with high hopes of happiness and job satisfaction.

The latter had been easy enough to find, but over recent months he'd been in a desolate kind of limbo, as if he didn't belong anywhere or to anyone. It had been a phone call out of the blue that had brought about the decision to return to Devon.

The man who hadn't smiled once during the flight hadn't gone unobserved by some of the female passengers. He was an attractive member of the opposite sex. A big man with a lived-in sort of face, dark russet hair above cool hazel eyes, and a physique that lots of men would die for.

But for any of them who had smiled in his direction, or tried to chat to relieve the tedium of the flight, the verdict had been that he was an unsociable character, and Harry knew they were right. It was what he'd become, and he didn't give a damn.

The last thing he wanted to do was make small talk to strangers. He'd already told the woman who had persuaded him to return to Bluebell Cove that he didn't want to be met at the airport. It wasn't as if he didn't know where he was bound for. He'd lived there for the first thirty-two years of his life.

It was a couple of days after the Lomax family had flown to France and midnight was approaching. Marcus was asleep in his cot in the smaller of the two bedrooms of the apartment, and Phoebe was up a ladder in the sitting room, her long brown hair stuffed inside an old sun hat and wearing a pair of her brother-in-law's cast-off dungarees.

She was painting the ceiling in an attempt to brighten up the place when she heard footsteps on the stairs that led up from the surgery. She became still, with the brush dangling loosely from her hand. Either there was an intruder in the building or...

It had only been that morning she'd discovered that the new head of the practice was going to be living across the landing from her in the second of the two apartments above the surgery. For days on end, the departure of the much-loved and respected Ethan Lomax had dominated every conversation among surgery staff and villagers alike. In contrast, the arrival of his replacement had been spoken of only rarely, so when the senior practice nurse had mentioned casually that he would be moving into the other apartment, it had come as a shock to her. She'd groaned inwardly at the thought of how embarrassing it could turn out to be.

Phoebe knew he'd been employed at The Tides Practice some years ago, so wouldn't be a stranger to everyone, but he would be to her. Why wasn't he moving into somewhere more salubrious? she'd thought uncomfortably. The last thing she wanted was to be coming across him every time she opened her door.

She'd asked if he was bringing a family with him and had been told that he was a widower without children. So at least there would only be just the one person living across from her, which was some slight relief. And now, if the noise on the stairs *wasn't* an intruder, it would seem that he'd arrived. But she had to be sure before she called it a day and went to bed.

Putting the chain on and opening the door a crack, Phoebe peered out onto the landing. Deciding that the man in designer jeans and a smart jacket who was entering the opposite apartment fitted the role of new senior partner rather than burglar, she started to close the door quietly to avoid being observed. He turned suddenly, as if aware that he was being watched, and said, 'Hello, there.'

She opened the door a fraction wider and said through the crack, 'I heard you come up the stairs and was just checking who it was before I went to bed.' Unable to step out and face him in her ghastly get-up, Phoebe closed the door and locked it in one movement. Then, leaning against it limply, she thought she hadn't handled *that* very well.

But she was too tired to dwell on it—her arms ached from the painting and it had been a long day, with some of her calls way out in the countryside. She was in no mood to get excited about the new arrival, even though she had noted when peering through the crack that he was quite something as attractive men went.

But so was Darren, and ever since he'd disappeared from her life she'd agreed that the old saying 'handsome is as handsome does' often applied to good-looking men. Even though she'd survived the hurt *he'd* inflicted on her, if she never saw him again she wouldn't complain.

They'd lived together in London, when he'd been a rising star, determined to get to the top in a big city bank. She'd always been supportive of his career ambitions but had never expected them to come before starting a family. A child to love and care for had been something she'd been looking forward to so much, and she hadn't been prepared for his reaction when she'd fallen pregnant.

They'd discussed starting a family a few times and she'd noted that his interest had been lukewarm, but had assumed that once Darren held his child in his arms, he would be lost in wonderment.

Instead, to her horror and dismay he'd gone berserk at the news, insisting he wanted to get to the top in his profession before lumbering himself with kids. He'd then suggested that she have an abortion. That had been a step too far and, heartbroken, she'd given in her notice at the London medical practice where she'd been employed as a district nurse.

Leaving him unrepentant, she'd moved to be near her sister and brother-in-law, her only relatives, and had filed for divorce. Clearly marriage to a man whose career meant more to him than his unborn child had been a big mistake. She and Darren hadn't spoken since and were not likely to.

She'd written to tell him he had a son when Marcus had been born but had received no response. A phone call from one of the girls at the bank had explained why. He was living with the daughter of the chairman of his bank and soon there would be wedding bells. It was to be hoped that wife number two was aware of his aversion to family life, she'd thought wryly, but was sure that a grandchild for the chairman of the bank would be much more welcome than one whose mother was just a mere nurse.

When she'd taken off the dungarees and freed her hair from under the sun hat, Phoebe went to stand by her baby's cot. Marcus was sleeping in pink and gold perfection, and

planting a butterfly kiss on his smooth cheek Phoebe knew
that her ex-husband was the loser in all of this.

As he placed the large case he'd humped up the stairs
inside a small hallway, and closed the door behind him,
Harry thought, *What or who was that?*

The voice had been that of a woman, so had the big
brown eyes observing him warily through the narrow
opening. But there had been no hair visible, and he'd
caught a glimpse of what looked like paint-splashed
dungarees.

Not a very good beginning, Harry, he thought. His
aunt had abided by his wishes that there should be no
fuss on his arrival, but clearly hadn't thought to inform
him that he was going to have a strange neighbour.

He'd let himself into the surgery building, which he'd
last seen five years ago, with one thought in mind—to
get some sleep. The last thing he wanted was to still be
under the covers the next morning when he was due to
make his first appearance in the practice.

Putting from his mind how the privacy of his arrival
had been butted into by some cautious, brown-eyed
gremlin, he went to check out the kitchen before having
a shower and then going to bed.

There was food in the fridge and the kitchen cup-
boards—fresh bread, scones, milk, cheese, bacon,
eggs, and in pride of place a large carton of the clotted cream so famous in Devon and Cornwall.

He smiled for the first time in hours. His aunt,
Barbara Balfour, who had instigated his return to
Bluebell Cove, might be less of the woman she had

once been, but she would definitely be behind all this, he thought.

Then he explored the bedroom, and came upon the welcome sight of a big double bed made up with fresh linen. When he crossed over to the bedroom window, a winter moon was shining above the village. In the distance, the lights of the house on the headland where his aunt and uncle lived glistened and flickered in the fresh breeze that had been the first thing he'd been aware of as he'd paid off the taxi that had brought him from the airport. As he'd breathed it in, it had been like wine after the dry heat of the country he'd just left.

The next morning, the travel alarm that Harry had brought with him fulfilled its function and he was down in the surgery before eight o'clock, just as the cleaner was leaving. By the time he'd introduced himself to the rosy-cheeked, middle-aged woman called Sarah, who informed him smilingly that her next task was to see her young ones safely off to school, and had renewed his acquaintance with the familiar layout of the surgery, the other staff were arriving.

Dr Leo Fenchurch, his second in command, was the first to arrive, followed by three practice nurses, three receptionists, a practice manager and the local midwife, who was based at the surgery.

As half past eight was approaching, and the surgery would soon be open to the public, Harry called them all together to have a brief chat and introduce himself. Picking up on the atmosphere, which was slightly lukewarm, he thought that Ethan Lomax was going to be a hard act to follow.

The two men had been friends and colleagues in the past, working at The Tides Medical Practice after qualifying. At that time the formidable Barbara Balfour, his aunt, had been senior partner, and no doubt would still have held that position if her health hadn't started to fail.

He had severed his connection with the place when he'd married Cassie, but Ethan had stayed on until recently when he'd given in to his wife's wishes and the family had moved to France.

Following in Ethan's footsteps didn't daunt him. He had no qualms about the job—he knew his own strengths when it came to that. More challenging were the other reasons behind his return. It was a case of hoping that somehow, in Bluebell Cove, he would find some ease from the grief that had been dragging him down during the last six months.

Harry looked over his new staff keenly—after all, they were the nucleus of the practice, so named because of the stretch of golden sand below the cliffs and the surging sea that came and went endlessly into the cove.

As it was his first morning, he was not aware that there was someone missing.

But while he'd been chatting to the cleaner, Phoebe had come down the back staircase that led to the apartments with Marcus in her arms, and had driven off to the nursery where he would be cared for until she'd finished her calls.

His baby buggy was in the boot, where it had been left the day before. In the short time that it took to unload it and pass her little one into the arms of Beth Dryden, who was in charge of Tiny Toes Nursery, Phoebe was acutely aware that she was running late. Marcus, who was teething, hadn't wanted his breakfast or been his usual contented little self while she'd been dressing him, all of which had been time consuming.

But he was smiling now, she thought thankfully. After explaining his earlier teething fretfulness to Beth and receiving her reassurance that she would give him some breakfast and would keep an eye on him, she drove back to the surgery where an explanation for her lateness was due to the new senior partner. After last night's uncomfortable few moments of meeting, she wasn't looking forward to it.

If it had been Ethan she wouldn't have needed to explain. He'd been kindness itself to her ever since she'd joined the practice—even while she'd been on leave after Marcus's birth he'd still kept in touch. Harry Balfour, however, was an unknown quantity.

When she hurried into the surgery he was standing by Reception on the phone. Lucy, the senior practice nurse, said in a low voice, 'Harry's talking to Ethan. What kept you Phoebe, baby's teeth?'

'Yes, he was really fretful this morning, today of all days.'

The elderly nurse nodded and looking towards the newcomer said, 'He's very sombre, not the guy he used to be. Harry was always happy and carefree but, then, he *has* just lost his wife in tragic circumstances. Why don't you go and sort out your calls while he's on the phone and introduce yourself to him afterwards?'

'Harry, it's Ethan here,' the voice at the other end of the line had said when the receptionist handed him the phone. 'Clearly you've arrived safely and are already on the job, so every good wish from all of us here! It gives me a good feeling to know that you are taking up where I left off.'

'It's kind of you to say so,' Harry told him. 'I'd forgotten how lovely it is here. With regard to the practice, I've gathered all the staff together and introduced myself. I'm also very happy with the apartment, it's really smart. Am I right in thinking that my aunt has been involved in the make-over?'

'Yes, you are,' was the reply. 'Have you spoken to Barbara yet?'

'No. I intend to go to Four Winds House this evening if she and Keith don't show up before then.'

'Fine, but prepare yourself for a shock when you see her. Barbara's mobility is very limited and her heart isn't good. She's being treated for that by her new son-in-law, my friend Lucas Devereux, who is a heart surgeon. He and your cousin Jenna were married a year ago and have a baby girl called Lily.'

They'd continued the conversation for a little while longer and by the time Harry was replacing the receiver Phoebe was almost ready to set off on her home visits. First, however, she needed to make herself known to him in a proper manner after the strangeness of their first meeting, if it could be described as that.

He'd turned away from the Reception desk and as she moved towards him, the first thing he observed about her was the pale perfection of her skin. After spending years in a country where women were often very tanned by the sun, it was breathtaking.

Trimly dressed in the dark blue dress of her calling, Phoebe had taken her hair off her face into a neat coil held back by a comb. It wasn't until his gaze met hers that Harry thought there couldn't be two pairs of big brown eyes like that on the surgery premises. But that was the only similarity to the ragamuffin who'd been watching him unlock the door of his new home the night before. He put out a feeler.

'I think we've already met,' he said dryly, before she could explain why she was late. 'Am I right?'

'Yes, you are,' she told him, holding out a smooth, ringless hand for him to shake. 'I'm Phoebe Howard, the district nurse attached to the practice. Last night you caught me in the middle of painting the ceiling—I'm afraid when I heard you coming up the stairs I had to check as it's been rather spooky with just the two of us up there.'

And what was that supposed to mean? he wondered. If she was living with a husband or partner one might expect that they would do the decorating. Yet a vision of Cassie came to mind. She'd been good at that sort of thing, said it kept her occupied when he was working long hours at the hospital where he'd been employed for most of his time in Australia.

She used to have a go at anything, had often been reckless, but it had seemed as if she'd had a charmed life. Until one Saturday morning, when they'd had words because he hadn't been free to do what she'd wanted which was to try out her new car.

He'd been on duty at the hospital, and as far as he'd been concerned, his patients had come first, so Cassie had set off in a huff and while driving along a remote road in the outback, the driver of a large oncoming truck had swerved into her path. The consequences had been disastrous—he'd lost his wife in a matter of seconds.

The accident had been six months ago and coming to terms with it had been grim. Thankfully they'd had no children to be left motherless. They'd both been of a like mind, that there had been plenty of time for that, though for very different reasons.

On Cassie's part, it had been because she hadn't been quite ready to give up what she'd seen as her freedom. But on Harry's part, it had been because he'd had a baby brother who had died from a genetic illness when he had been just a child himself. Yet, he'd been old enough to experience the frightening feeling of loss, and growing up as the remaining child of grief-stricken parents, the fear of bringing a child into the world and then losing it always lurked in the recesses of his mind.

He'd seen his mother weeping and his father's perma-nently sad expression, and had thought that it was better not to have babies if the angels were going to take them up to heaven.

'I'm sorry I was late arriving,' the young nurse beside him was saying apologetically, and bringing his thoughts back to bear on why he was standing there, Harry said briskly, 'That's OK, just as long as it isn't a habit.'

Hoping that in days to come the new senior partner wouldn't feel that unavoidable came into the same category as a habit, Phoebe managed a strained smile. Then picking up the case that held what she needed for her patients, she went quickly out through the main door of the surgery.

Her first call of the day was to the home of a man who had just been diagnosed with insulin-dependent diabetes. Frank Atkinson was a newly retired forestry worker and she'd explained the procedure of injecting himself the previous day. Now she was on her way to check if he was having any problems.

Always a frightening ordeal at first, most people soon got into a routine and accepted the inevitability of it. Sure enough, when she arrived at a pretty thatched cottage on the coast road she found that he had coped and was less agitated than on the day before.

As was often the case, there was hospitality on offer. His wife Betty, who knew something of the circumstances of the young district nurse, had coffee and shortbread waiting when Phoebe had finished dealing with her husband.

'I won't say no,' she said thankfully. 'My little one is teething and was really out of sorts this morning, so I didn't have time to have any breakfast. I mustn't linger, though. We have a new doctor in charge of the practice and I've already made a poor start by being late, so don't want to transgress any further! He has the look of a man who doesn't suffer fools gladly.'

'Surely he will make allowances for you being a single mother,' Betty protested.

'I suppose he might if he knew, but we only met last night. He doesn't yet know I have a child, and when he does I won't be expecting any favours. It wouldn't be fair to the rest of the staff.'

When she was ready to go, Betty walked to the bottom of the garden path with her. Wistfully she said, 'Under any other circumstances, Frank would have been holding forth about trees this morning—they're his favourite subject—but not any more. I used to weary of it sometimes, but now I'd give anything to hear about the oaks and the elms and the sycamores.'

'I'm sure that you will be hearing about them again soon, Betty,' Phoebe told her consolingly. As she left, she said reassuringly, 'I'll call again tomorrow and for as long as it takes for Frank to be completely confident when injecting the insulin.'

There was another new patient on her list of calls, and as she pulled up in front of a shop across from the harbour that sold fishing tackle, it was clear that its owner had been on the lookout for her. The moment she stepped out of the car, a young blonde guy with a beard came striding out and without wasting a second said, 'I'm Jake Stephenson and the patient is my young nephew Rory. He's staying with me for a while as both his parents are in hospital after a car crash.

'Rory was hurt too, but to a lesser degree. However, he has a nasty leg wound that I've been told he mustn't put any weight on for the time being. The hospital phoned the surgery to ask for a district nurse to come and dress the wound, and keep an eye on it.'

He was leading the way back into the shop and Phoebe followed, not having been able to get a word in so far. But she was used to anxiety creating a non-stop spate of words, and had listened carefully to what he had been saying.

'Here he is,' he said, opening the door of a sitting room at the back of the shop. A young teenage boy, with a bandaged leg resting on a stool in front of him, looked up from the computer game he was playing for a moment and then went back to it.

'Switch that off for a moment, Rory,' the harassed uncle ordered, and the boy obeyed reluctantly.

'Hello, there,' Phoebe said. 'I've come to have a look at your leg, Rory.'

He nodded sullenly but didn't speak, and kneeling beside him she gently removed the dressing.

When the injury was revealed she saw that a deep gash had been stitched, most likely from when he'd first been taken to A and E after the crash. However, the skin around it over quite a large area had been scraped off and was looking sore and weepy, so she hesitated before using more of the cream he'd been given by the hospital.

'It's my dad's fault,' the youngster grumbled as he looked down at his leg. 'He always drives too fast. I hate him. Supposing I can't play footie again!'

'Shush,' she said gently. 'It would have to be much worse than this for that to happen. I'm going to ask one of the doctors from the surgery to come and look at your leg.' Signalling to Jake to go back into the shop so they could talk, she smiled at Rory reassuringly and followed his uncle as he led the way out of the room.

'If only Rory wasn't so difficult,' he said when they were out of his hearing. 'He isn't usually like this.'

'He's feeling frightened and insecure,' she told him. 'The poor boy has been involved in a car crash, which must have been terrifying. Even though from the sound of it his parents were the ones most seriously hurt, all he can see at the moment is what it did to him.'

She was reaching for her mobile phone. 'I'm going to see if Dr Fenchurch is back from his rounds. I need a second opinion before I treat the leg again with the same procedure as before.'

'I'm afraid Leo isn't here,' Millie on Reception told her when she answered the phone. 'His car broke down as he was leaving his last house call, and he's out there waiting for the breakdown services to show up. But Dr Balfour is here, and if you give us the address, he says he'll be right with you.'

Phoebe almost groaned out loud. Since he'd arrived back on his home ground, she'd met the abrupt man twice in the space of twenty-four hours. And each time she *hadn't* come out of it as the epitome of efficiency.

He was bound to think that she should be able to deal with this sort of problem with her eyes shut, she thought rebelliously. But Rory was an injured youngster who was frightened and hurting because of his family's careless-ness, and if he couldn't rely on his father to do the right thing by him, he could rely on her. She knew he needed a second opinion on that leg of his so grudgingly, she gave the address.

When Harry Balfour came striding into the cluttered shop premises ten minutes later, he found Phoebe drinking the coffee that a grateful Jake Stephenson had insisted on offering her, and he frowned. It didn't look much like an emergency at first glance, he thought. But she put the cup down immediately and took him into the sitting room where Rory was, and he had to change his assumption.

As soon as he saw the boy's leg, he knew that the district nurse had been right to send for a doctor.

'How long is it since they sent Rory home from the hospital?' he asked as he scrutinised the wound.

'Last night,' Jake told him.

'How long since the accident?

'A couple of days before. His parents are still in there, both with concussion, broken legs and pelvic injuries. Once they'd seen to Rory's leg, the doctors decided that he would be better out of hospital and sent him to me, his uncle, for the time being.'

So far Phoebe hadn't spoken. Harry Balfour had that effect on her, making her clam up when she should be showing him that she was no pushover. When he turned to her after he'd finished examining the leg, he found himself looking into her wide brown gaze and seeing a defiant kind of wariness there.

Yet not for long. It quickly turned to surprise when he said crisply, 'You were right to send for one of us. I'm of the opinion that Rory is allergic to the antiseptic cream they gave him at the hospital. Although it is highly recommended by most doctors, I have heard of the occasional case where the patient has had an allergic reaction to one of its components, so we will change the ointment and check the condition of the injury once again after twenty-four hours.'

He was writing out a prescription as he spoke and said to Phoebe, 'I see there's a chemist two doors away. If you would like to pop in there and get this made up, perhaps Mr. Stephenson might have another cup of coffee on offer before I depart.'

CHAPTER TWO

SO HARRY BALFOUR was human after all, Phoebe thought while the chemist was making up the prescription. Not as approachable as that nice guy Jake maybe, but not quite as scary and abrupt as she'd at first thought. Although, of course, it was early days. He didn't yet know there was a teething infant just across the landing, and his reaction to that might depend on just how much he valued his sleep!

When she returned to the shop, he'd departed, leaving a message to say he'd gone back to the practice to prepare for the second surgery of the day. So once she had put the new antiseptic cream on Rory's leg and placed a clean dressing over the infected area, she bade uncle and nephew goodbye, promising to return the next day to check on the effects of the new cream, and proceeded to the next housebound patient on her list.

She was back at the surgery by half past three. After updating her patients' records, Phoebe was about to depart just after four when Harry came out of his consulting room. Observing that she was dressed for going out into the cold January day once more, he asked, 'Have you had another callout?'

She smiled weakly. 'Er, no. I finish at four. Ethan agreed that I could.'

'I see,' he commented. 'And you didn't think fit to inform me of an arrangement you'd made with my predecessor?'

'It is in my records, Dr Balfour.'

'Maybe, but I only arrived back in Bluebell Cove late last night. Since I presented myself here in the surgery at a very early hour this morning, there have been many things I needed to get to know. As you might imagine, checking staff records is low on my list of priorities at the moment.'

'I'm sorry. It was remiss of me not to mention it,' she said, uncomfortable in the knowledge that he hadn't the slightest idea why she was allowed to finish early, and probably wasn't going to be over the moon when he found out.

Ethan had agreed to her finishing at four each day when she'd started work at the end of her maternity leave, and she'd been most grateful—it had meant she'd been able to collect Marcus from the nursery earlier than she'd expected. The normal finishing time for surgery staff was six-thirty, so the early finish gave her an extra two and a half hours each weekday evening with her baby. It had meant less pay but time with Marcus came first.

'So you'd better be off, then, hadn't you, if that's the arrangement?' Harry said into the middle of the awkward moment. 'We'll have a chat regarding your hours when I've had the chance to settle in properly.'

She nodded and went hurrying off. Watching her go, he wondered what it was about her that brought out the worst in him.

Was it because she was so strangely beautiful...and alive?

When Phoebe arrived at the nursery the report on Marcus was that he'd been a little fretful but otherwise fine. She breathed a sigh of relief. There was no indication that the tooth that was bothering him had come through but at least, from what Beth had said, he hadn't been crying all day.

Teething, walking, talking...they were all natural processes in the normal growth of a child, she thought, but could still prove to be times of anxiety for the parent until they had been safely achieved.

From half past six onwards, after the surgery had closed, Phoebe was listening for the footsteps on the stairs, but all was silent. She wondered if Harry was still down there catching up with more information regarding the running of the surgery, or if he had gone out somewhere.

Marcus had been asleep for hours and she was about to slide under the covers herself when she heard him come upstairs. It was gone ten o'clock, and Phoebe felt herself relaxing. They may not have had the best of introductions, the single mother and the abrupt widower, but it was good to feel that she wasn't on her own above the sprawling surgery complex.

* * *

Barbara Balfour had rung Harry late that morning to pass on a word of welcome, and to enquire if everything had been in order both below and above when he'd arrived the night before.

'Yes,' he'd told her, 'everything is fine.'

'So will you come and dine with us tonight, Harry?' she'd said. 'We are both so pleased to have you back here in Bluebell Cove. It seems a long time since you and Jenna used to take your surfboards down to the beach for hours on end.'

'That's because it *is* a long time, Aunt Barbara,' he'd said with one of his rare smiles. 'It seems strange to think of Jenna married with a baby.'

'Strange or not, it is so,' he'd been assured. 'Her husband Lucas is a cardiac surgeon. I'm one of his patients, as a matter of fact. Our son-in-law is also a great friend of Ethan. He and Francine are godparents to our little Lily.'

'It all sounds very happy and cosy.' he'd said lightly, relieved that she hadn't been able to witness the envy in his expression.

Nonetheless, he'd accepted Barbara's invitation. Having been warned by Ethan about the physical deterioration of his hostess, he had concealed his dismay when he saw her, while at the same time taking note that the razor-sharp mind was still very much in evidence.

After a pleasant evening with his relations, he'd left, promising Barbara that he would keep her informed about what was going on at the practice. At the moment of departure he'd paused and asked, 'Did you know that the other apartment is occupied, Aunt Barbara?'

Her expression had said she hadn't known and her husband Keith said, 'It will be an arrangement that Ethan will have agreed to before he left—probably a member of the staff.'

'That's correct,' Harry had told him. 'Her name is Phoebe Howard, she's the district nurse.'

The retired doctor had shaken her head. 'Although I take a great interest in the practice, I'm afraid I don't know every member of staff, Harry. She must be some-one new.'

'Yes, I suppose that could be it,' he'd agreed, and after saying his farewells had disappeared into the winter night.

And now he was back at the apartment and wonder-ing if history would repeat itself, if the door opposite would be opened a crack to observe him. But it remained closed and there was silence all around, which was how he preferred it to be, wasn't it?

It was two o'clock in the morning and there was silence no longer. He'd been awakened by a strange sound and was lying wide eyed against the pillows, trying to iden-tify it. It wasn't a cat yowling out on the tiles, he told himself, or someone who'd had too much to drink break-ing into song as they went past the surgery building.

He sat up suddenly. It was the loud cry of a baby that was shattering the peace and he was out of bed in a flash, quickly throwing on a robe.

The door opposite was still closed when he went out onto the landing but he had no doubt about where the cry was coming from. Phoebe had a baby in there and from the noise issuing forth, it was not a happy one. The doctor in him simply couldn't not check if everything was all right.

The crying stopped for a moment and he knocked on the door, but it still remained closed. In case the district nurse had a husband or partner with her who might be bristling at the invasion of their privacy, he called, 'I've no wish to intrude but can I help?'

There was no response and he was in the process of knocking again when the door opened suddenly and he almost fell on top of Phoebe. The baby she was holding observed him with tear-drenched brown eyes as she said apologetically, 'I'm sorry we've disturbed you, Dr Balfour. I'm afraid that Marcus is teething.'

He glanced around the room and still poised on the threshold asked, 'Are you living alone up here with a young baby?'

Phoebe hesitated and as if on cue the infant in her arms began to cry again. She stepped back reluctantly to let him in and said, 'Yes, I'm afraid there are just the two of us. If you want to help, could you possibly hold Marcus for a moment while I make him a bottle? It usually soothes him back to sleep. And, Dr Balfour, the reason I didn't tell you I had a baby was exactly because of nights like this. I didn't want us to disturb your privacy, but I should have known better.'

Harry had stepped inside and was observing her doubtfully as she held out the baby for him to take from her. She smiled and told him, 'He won't bite you. He's only been protesting because he's teething. Look, he's smiling now.' He looked down at the small warm body that he was now holding close to his. Sure enough, there was a little smile coming in his direction from the child with the same pale skin and wide brown gaze as his mother.

She was moving towards the kitchen to make the bottle, and Harry said in a low voice, 'Do I take it that his father isn't around?'

'Yes,' she said quietly, not looking at him. 'We're divorced.'

He nodded, and looking down at the child in his arms said wryly, 'And this is the reason why you finish early? Why on earth didn't you tell me that?'

'Yes, Marcus is the reason,' she said steadily. 'I take him to a nursery in the village before I start at the surgery on weekdays and have to pick him up at four o'clock. I suppose one of the reasons for me not telling you was because I don't want anyone seeing me as disadvantaged. I chose the kind of life I'm living and have no regrets. It was Ethan's suggestion that I finish early and I was hardly going to refuse when it gave me some extra time with my son.'

'So how long have you lived here?'

'Only since New Year. My maternity leave was up at the end of December. I'd lived with my sister and brother-in-law before that,' and with a tired smile. 'So now you have the story of my life.'

'Not entirely, I would imagine,' he said dryly. He looked down at Marcus who was getting ready for another weeping bout. 'If that bottle is ready, now might be the moment to produce it.' With a feeling that he was out of his depth and had served his purpose, he said, 'If you're sure he's going to settle, I'll leave you to it.'

'Yes, we'll be fine,' she said hurriedly. 'I feel that I've been taking advantage of your good nature, Dr Balfour.'

'I haven't got a good nature to take advantage of,' he informed her shortly and then pausing in the doorway, amazed himself by saying, 'Before I go, why don't *I* make *you* a warm drink? Coffee maybe?'

'Er, yes, please, that would be lovely, and do make one for yourself,' Phoebe said meekly, wanting to pinch herself to make sure she wasn't dreaming. She couldn't remember what it felt like to have someone do something for her, and of all people it was the unpredictable new head of the practice who was waiting on her in the middle of the night.

Marcus had been fed and changed, and was now sleeping peacefully in his cot. On the point of finally going back to his own apartment, Harry said, 'Just one thing— if ever you need any help like tonight, feel free to call on me.

'I would rather you did that than me having to lie there imagining you struggling on your own. And by the way, Nurse Howard, why is this place so much less attractive than mine?'

'I'm not sure,' she told him, 'but it isn't going to be like this for long! And I will only ever disturb you if it's an emergency—when we move house we can't choose our neighbours, can we? They come as part of the package.'

Harry wondered if that was in the form of an apology, or letting him know that she wasn't all that keen on having him living so close.

But if she'd been expecting a reply, there was none forthcoming and as tiredness took hold of her, she wished him goodnight and bolted the door behind him.

When she went back to bed exhaustion was there, but not sleep. Her mind kept going over what had turned out to be the strangest of days. It has been full of highs and lows between Harry Balfour and herself, then had ended with him knocking on her door and offering to help with Marcus. She'd been so tired and frayed at the edges she'd welcomed him with open arms and thrust her little one at him.

Yet there was no way she was going to take him up on his offer by using him as a standby in times of stress. The odds were that he wouldn't have taken the apartment across the landing if he'd known that his neighbours were going to be a single mother and her baby.

Despite his offer of help, he hadn't exactly seemed very comfortable around Marcus. Lucy, the elderly practice nurse, had told her on the day he had been due to arrive that he hadn't any family to bring with him, which maybe explained his reluctance to hold Marcus and his eagerness to be off once he had been satisfied that calm had been restored.

Yet he'd lingered long enough to make her the hot drink she'd been gasping for, and had made one for himself, as she'd suggested. But those had been things unconnected with her child... A last thought struck as her eyelids began to droop. Maybe his reaction on discovering there was a baby living only feet away wasn't all that strange, as it clearly wouldn't be every man's idea of heaven.

Across the landing Harry's thoughts were moving along different channels. Seated in a chair by the window, looking out bleakly at a starlit winter sky, he was remembering a time long ago when a baby precious to him and his parents had been lost, and how nothing had ever been the same afterwards.

Only small himself, he'd been left lonely and unloved while they'd tried to cope with their grief by spending all their time in their business, running stables in Bluebell Cove. Ever since, he'd been reluctant to take on the responsibility of bringing a child into a world where nothing was certain and loss could bring with it such pain and loneliness.

So family life wasn't something he was familiar with due to his childhood. Marriage to a woman who had been in no hurry to start a family had also left his wariness of it unchanged.

Yet Phoebe across the landing had opted for it without the support of a husband or partner and seemed content, so which of them had the right idea?

Breakfast and getting Marcus to the nursery went smoothly the next morning, and Phoebe was at the surgery in good time, although with an uncomfortable feeling inside whenever she thought about her nocturnal meeting with Harry.

She shuddered to think what she must have looked like in a crumpled cotton nightdress with an old robe over it and her hair all over the place, yet it didn't really matter. He'd been in her apartment for just one thing and there'd been nothing sensual about it. He'd come to assist in the hope of bringing back the peace that had prevailed before Marcus had begun his tantrum, and she'd do well to remember that!

Leo Fenchurch, the other doctor in the practice, had been out on an early call and appeared while she was making the usual big pot of tea for the staff before the day commenced. He brought a blast of cold air in with him and while warming his hands around a mug of the welcoming brew he said, 'So, what do you think of the new guy, Phoebe?'

He was a fair-haired six-footer with a charm that appealed to most women, but not to her she thought. He was an excellent doctor but a bit lightweight for her to succumb to his charms.

'I'm not sure,' she said in answer to his question. 'I feel that he isn't going to be an easy person to get to know, that he is very much his own man. Yet I'm sure he will be good for the practice, even if he can be somewhat unpredictable on occasion.' *And of that I have on-the-spot experience*, she thought.

'But, Leo, we have to remember that Harry has lost his wife in tragic circumstances. I'm not sure how, but it was an accident of some kind, and for a marriage to end like that must have been horrendous.

'Mine fell apart because of a huge divide in our priorities, but we at least we had a choice, not like Harry.'

'Wow!' he exclaimed. 'That summing-up comes after him having spent just a short time among us? You must have seen more of him than we have.'

She wasn't going to enlighten him on that and almost dropped the mug she was holding when Harry's voice said from behind her in the passage, 'Is there any tea on offer, Nurse Howard?'

As she reached for the teapot, Phoebe was praying that he hadn't heard her discussing him with Leo. It would be just too embarrassing if he had, but his expression was serene enough, and once she'd poured him the tea, he returned to his room without further comment. As the rest of the staff were appearing in varying degrees of haste for their early brew, she tried to put the incident out of her mind.

She wouldn't have been able to if she'd seen Harry's expression as he sat gazing into space behind his desk with the tea untouched. It would seem that little Baby Bunting's mother had him well and truly catalogued, he thought dryly.

Thankfully his visit to her apartment in the middle of the night hadn't been mentioned—it would have gone around the surgery like wildfire! Noting that it was almost time for the day to start, he went out into Reception to have a word with Phoebe before she left.

She was halfway through the main door when he called her back. He saw her shoulders stiffen and almost smiled. What did she think he wanted her for, to tell her that he'd heard what she'd said to Leo?

'Did you manage to get some sleep after I left?' he asked in a low voice.

'Er…yes,' she replied, looking around her quickly to make sure no one was near enough to jump to any wrong conclusions. 'Marcus was fine this morning. It seems as if the tooth might have come through.'

He was smiling and she thought how different he looked when he did, but a second later he was the man in charge as he said, 'You've got young Rory down for a visit, I hope.'

'He's top of my list, Dr Balfour,' she said stiffly. 'If I am still concerned about his leg I will be asking for your presence or that of Dr Fenchurch.'

'Good,' he said briskly, as if he hadn't picked up on the drop in temperature. 'Hope you have a good day after a not-so-good night. I see that the waiting room is filling up so must go.' And off he went, wishing that he hadn't come over as quite so bossy with Phoebe. He wouldn't be surprised if she had him labelled as a control freak!

Conversely, as Phoebe drove the short distance to the fishing-tackle shop she was thinking that the man was only doing his job. So why had she let him get to her like that? He'd been kind and supportive in the middle of the night, even though she could tell that he wasn't used to babies. It was ungrateful of her to take offence at what, to Harry, would just be part of the job.

The infection around the sutures on Rory's leg had improved overnight, and with it the boy's mood. As she changed the dressing, with his uncle looking on anxiously, Phoebe told him, 'Make sure that he takes all the antibiotics he was given when he left the hospital, Jake.

That and the different kind of ointment we're using now
should do the trick.'

He breathed a sigh of relief. 'The last thing I would
want to tell my sister is that her boy isn't well, so that's
good news, Nurse.'

'How are his parents progressing?' she questioned.

'Not bad, but they have a way to go yet before
Hunter's Hill will be ready to send them home. So it's
just the two of us for a while, isn't it, Rory?' he said to
his nephew, who was still in his pyjamas.

'Yes, Uncle Jake,' he chirped. 'And don't forget,
as soon as my leg is all right, we're going out in your
boat.'

'There's no chance of me forgetting,' was the teasing
reply. 'You won't let me!'

Jake turned to Phoebe. 'How about a coffee before
you go, Nurse?'

She shook her head. 'No, thanks just the same, I've
got a rather long list of patients to see and must be on
my way.'

He was smiling. 'If I can't make you a drink, how
about letting me take you for a sail when this young
fellow is well enough to come along?'

'I don't think so,' she told him gently. 'You wouldn't
want a young baby on the boat.'

'So you're married,' he said disappointedly.

'No. I'm a single mother,' she explained, and could
tell from his expression that a possible relationship had
just gone down the drain. Yet who could blame him? She
couldn't help but think it would take a lot for a man to

be willing to fill the gap of a father in the life of another man's child, however nice he was.

She'd also only met Jake for the first time the day before. It would take longer than that for her to want to know him better or introduce him to her son. But as a vision of Harry Balfour awkwardly holding Marcus safe and secure in his arms came to mind, she thought that she'd only known *him* for a similar length of time, yet she would trust him with her child.

When she arrived at her next call, pulling up in front of the biggest farmhouse in the area, Phoebe was amazed to see the man who had been in her thoughts getting out of the brand-new red convertible he'd had delivered to the surgery that morning. The question was immediately there in her mind—was he checking up on her?

It seemed that he wasn't. Harry was already ringing the bell and called across to her, 'Well timed. We have an emergency.'

She was out of her car in a flash and hurried to the door, wondering what could be wrong at Wheatlands Farm.

She visited the place every week to put a fresh dressing on a varicose ulcer that was plaguing old George Enderby, the patriarch of the family. As far as she was aware, that was the only thing wrong with the cheerful old guy, but if what Harry was saying was correct...

'Is it George that you're here about?' she asked as footsteps pounded towards them from inside the house.

He shook his head. 'No. A call came through to the

surgery to say his daughter-in-law Pamela had fallen downstairs early this morning and almost knocked herself senseless with a crack to her head. She was soon back working on the farm, until a few minutes ago when suddenly she didn't seem to know where she was.'

The door was being wrenched open as he spoke and George's son Ian was there, his face taut with anxiety.

'Thanks for coming so quickly, Harry,' he said urgently. 'I wasn't expecting us to be renewing our acquaintance so soon. Pamela is upstairs resting with a huge bump on her head and isn't very coherent.'

'So let's have a look, then,' he said briskly, adding to Phoebe, 'Come along, Nurse, you can see to your patient when we've sorted Mrs Enderby out.'

The swelling on Pamela Enderby's head was huge and soft to the touch and her eyes weren't functioning properly. Neither was her mind as Harry gently tried to get her to answer a few simple questions rationally.

Turning to her husband, he said in a low voice, 'There is almost certainly bleeding inside the skull.' He turned to Phoebe. 'Phone for an ambulance, Nurse, and stress the urgency, while I check the patient's heartbeat and pulse.'

She was about to confirm that the emergency services were hastening on their way when he said tightly, 'Pamela's gone into a coma.' He placed his stethoscope against her chest. 'There's no heartbeat! Get ready to resuscitate!'

Together they worked on the patient until the ambulance arrived and paramedics stepped in with a defibrillator and then a faint rising and falling of the injured woman's chest indicated that she was back with them.

Her husband had watched their efforts with tears streaming down his face and as the ambulance was leaving, with him by her side and a paramedic monitoring her heartbeat, he said raggedly, 'Whatever the outcome of this, I will never forget what the two of you did back there.'

Before they could reply, he was gone with flashing lights and sirens wailing to warn other road users that the vehicle was carrying someone seriously ill or injured.

'That was good teamwork, Phoebe,' Harry said with one of his rare smiles when it had disappeared from sight.

It registered that he'd actually said her name, but there was no time for further thought as elderly George, the patient she'd originally come to see, appeared beside them looking distraught and decidedly unsteady on his feet.

'I've kept out of the way,' he said breathing heavily. 'At my age I'm no good in a crisis. So what's the verdict, Harry?'

'Not too good at this moment, George,' the doctor told him gently. 'They will have to operate to control a brain haemorrhage. But she is still with us, so why don't you let me make you a cup of tea while Nurse Howard changes the dressing on your leg? Or would you prefer a brandy under the circumstances?'

'Yes, I would,' he replied. 'My heart isn't too good and the last thing my son needs is me cracking up at a time like this.' He was gazing out at the immaculate farm buildings and the land that belonged to them stretching as far as the eye could see. 'All of this is great, Harry,' he said brokenly, 'but it means nothing when a life is at stake.'

Harry nodded understandingly. The Enderbys were obviously very wealthy, but the old guy had his priorities right.

'Can I leave you to see to George?' he asked Phoebe. 'I left patients waiting to see me when I dashed over here.'

'Yes, of course,' she told him, adding as he turned to go, 'It was great working with you.'

The reluctant smile was back and she thought if he kept it up, he might actually manage a laugh one day. To her amazement he replied, 'It was good to have you assisting me, Nurse Howard.' And then he was gone to face the sighs and fidgets of those awaiting his presence in the surgery.

Having dealt with George's dressing and left him in the charge of the farm's housekeeper, Phoebe continued her home visits. When she arrived back at the surgery late in the afternoon, keen to see if the rapport between herself and Harry was still there or just a momentary thing, she found him closeted with one patient after another and it was still so when she left to pick Marcus up at the nursery.

With the tooth now through, he was back to his usual state of contentment, greeting her with a big smile and a happy gurgle, and in that moment the other part of her life took over. He was all she had, and if that was how it was always going to be, she wasn't going to complain. She'd made her choice when she split up with Darren and had no regrets about *that*.

CHAPTER THREE

WHILE Phoebe was feeding and bathing Marcus before settling him down for sleep, it was the same as the night before—she was listening for footsteps on the stairs to let her know that Harry's day at the practice was also over. This time she didn't have long to wait.

She heard him come up just as her baby's eyelids were closing, his dark lashes sweeping downwards and his small chest rising and falling steadily. Ridiculously, this time she *wanted* Harry to knock on her door so that she could see if the time they'd spent together with Pamela Enderby had really been as satisfying for him as it had been for her. His unexpected presence last night had also shown her another side to him that she wanted to see again.

Disappointed when she heard his door close behind him, she began to clear up after bathtime and was debating whether to get out the paint cans and brushes once more when the sound she'd been hoping for finally came.

While he'd been putting a ready meal in the oven to heat up, Harry had been debating whether it would be pushing it too far if he called on Phoebe again. Yet he felt he had to. It was going to be a frosty night and while her apartment had been warm enough the night before, it definitely was not as warm as his, and there was a spare mobile heater in his hall that he wanted to give her just in case. He wouldn't be able to settle if he hadn't offered it to her on such a cold night.

The last thing he'd expected when he'd told Ethan he'd like to move into one of the apartments had been the presence of a young single mother and child only a few feet away. The solitude that he'd sought wasn't materialising, but for some reason he didn't mind as much as he'd anticipated. As he crossed the landing with the heater, to his enormous surprise he even found himself hoping that he might get a glimpse of the smallest of the other apartment's occupants.

When Phoebe opened the door to him she was smiling, and it hit him again how unusually beautiful she was, with her clear, pale skin and wide hazel gaze that was observing him questioningly.

'Come in,' she said, stepping back while he humped the heavy appliance into her hall. As he straightened up to face her, she asked, 'What is that?'

'It's a heater,' he said in the brisk manner he used when not sure of himself. 'It is going to be a very cold night and I thought it might be welcome.'

'Where has it come from?'

'My place. I don't need it as my heating is excellent, and I noticed last night that yours is not so good. It just needs to be plugged into the electricity. So can I leave it with you?'

'Yes,' she said slowly, completely taken aback that her new boss should take the trouble to make sure that she and Marcus were warm enough on a bitter winter night. There was a lump in her throat and for an awful moment she felt she was going to weep in front of him, but she fought back the tears.

He wasn't to know that his small act of kindness had broken through the armour of self-sufficiency that she wore to protect herself from any more of the hurts that life might have in store for her.

'So where do you want it?' he was asking, observing her curiously.

'Here in the hall, I think,' she told him, desperately scrabbling for some composure. 'When I go to bed I'll leave all the doors open so that the extra heat can circulate.' Hoping that her surprise wasn't making her appear short on gratitude, she asked, 'Can I offer you a drink while you're here Dr Balfour? A glass of wine, perhaps, or something hot?'

'A glass of wine would be nice,' he said smoothly, much preferring a beer but feeling that it wouldn't be quite as suitable to the occasion. 'But I can't stay long. I have a meal in the oven.'

She nodded understandingly as she produced a bottle of white from the fridge, and as she was pouring it asked, 'Have we had any news on Pamela Enderby?'

'Yes,' he said. 'I rang the farm just before I came up and George said that she's in Theatre, having a huge haematoma drained. So far she's coping with it, but it is a serious situation and sadly I feel she will be lucky to come through it.'

Silence fell between them as they drank the wine, both lost in their own thoughts as they contemplated the strain that the Enderby family would be under tonight. In what seemed like no time at all he was getting to his feet and saying, 'I must go, Phoebe. And by the way, when we're not in the surgery it's Harry, OK?'

'Yes,' she said. 'I'll remember. And thanks again for the loan of the heater...er...Harry.'

Her obvious discomfort broke through the sadder thoughts about Pamela, and Harry found himself actually laughing. 'It will become easier as you keep saying it,' he promised. Then, on the point of leaving, he casually asked, 'Is Baby Bunting asleep?'

It was her turn to laugh. 'Need you ask?' she said, and added, amazing herself, 'Do you want to see for yourself?'

'Er...yes,' he replied hesitantly, 'just as long as you don't think it will disturb him.' Phoebe mentally kicked herself. Clearly he didn't want a repetition of last night, or maybe just a repetition of Marcus in general.

'No. Marcus never wakes up during the first few hours after going to sleep,' she informed him stiffly. 'It's in the middle of the night when he sometimes makes his presence felt, and that's only when he's teething. But the tooth that was bothering him is through now, so you should be spared any further nightly disturbances for a while.'

'What a beautiful child,' he said slowly as he turned away from the cherub in the cot, then almost as if he was speaking to himself, 'But they come with a lifetime's responsibility of caring, don't they? Always there is the fear in the mind of the loving parent that they might lose their child to illness or accident.'

Phoebe was observing him in surprise, shocked by his words and the desolation with which he'd uttered them. 'That's a rather downbeat way of looking at family life, isn't it?' she exclaimed. 'Surely you can't be speaking from experience?'

'No, of course not,' he said flatly. 'I was just express-ing a point of view that I'm sure you don't agree with.'

His bitterness sparked off Phoebe's anger. 'You're right. I don't. There are always risks in loving someone, whoever it might be. It can end in pain and despair, or it can be the most joyful thing in one's life, giving it a magical sense of purpose. And that is exactly what Marcus has given me.'

She gentled her tone, wondering how to explain to him that love was always worth the risk, no matter how scarred he felt by his past. 'I imagine that you are still hurting at the loss of your wife, Harry, and I can't tell you how sorry I was to hear about her death. But while you may think it's easy for me to talk, I really do believe what I've just said, and I'm sad for you that you don't feel the same.'

'Maybe we could discuss it another time.' he said abruptly. 'I'd better go. I can smell my meal burning from here. Goodnight, Phoebe.' And before she could reply he'd gone.

As he ate his solitary meal Harry was thinking that the woman across the landing must think him pathetic, hovering around her like Social Services and burbling on about the downside of family life.

His marriage to Cassie had been good in parts, but something of a roller-coaster ride. She'd been an extrovert, a risk-taker who'd thrived on excitement. Motherhood had never been high on her agenda, just as fatherhood had been low on his.

Maybe he should make it clear to Phoebe that his concern on her behalf was simply neighbourly, that he would have done the same for anyone he felt the heater would benefit. The fact that she had a child in her not-so-warm apartment had just made it seem the sensible thing to do.

But he'd come back to Bluebell Cove like a wounded animal to its lair, not to fraternise with the locals, and a staff member at that. So maybe he should play it cool with Phoebe from now on, and make sure he avoided bringing up such topics as love and family, which they clearly had wildly different opinions about.

Harry was nice under that brusque exterior, Phoebe thought as she felt the boost that the heater was giving to her very average central heating system. And her heart bled for the grief he'd suffered, and was clearly still struggling with.

Suddenly, instead of wishing that the other apartment was still unoccupied, she felt she was going to enjoy having Harry for a neighbour, but there was no way she would want him to think she saw him as anything other than that.

The responsibility of becoming a single mother had

been frightening while she'd been carrying Marcus and even more so during the first weeks after his birth. But with the help of Katie and Rob, who had been fantastic, and her own determination not to falter in the life she had chosen for herself, she was coping.

Every time she looked at the baby asleep in the next room, she knew she'd done the right thing. If it had been up to Darren, their child wouldn't have existed. The mere thought of that always brought her up with a jolt, especially when she was tired or discouraged at the end of a long day faced with a never-ending list of chores to do once Marcus was asleep.

But she wasn't so wrapped up in her restricted 'mother and child only' existence that she didn't recognise an attractive man when she saw one, and Harry was certainly that!

When she stepped onto the landing the next morning with Marcus in her arms, his door opened simultaneously and with a friendly smile she said, 'We stayed beautifully warm through the night, Harry. Thank you so much.'

There was no answering smile coming her way and she felt the colour rise beneath the smooth pale skin of her face as he said flatly, 'It was there, hanging about doing nothing, so don't feel indebted.'

Chastened, she increased her hold on Marcus and prepared to descend the stairs. In the same flat tone he said, 'Watch your step.'

She'd thought he might offer to carry Marcus down for her, or have a pleasant reply to her greeting, but instead it felt as if she'd entered some sort of cold zone and she didn't know why.

Unaware of his musings of the night before, she thought bleakly that it must be a double-edged warning—to watch her step on the stairs, and at the same time watch her step in her dealings with him, especially if she thought that the offer of the heater the night before had been an invitation to be all chummy. Was Sir Galahad going to turn out to be a Dr-Jekyll–Mr-Hyde sort of person just when she was warming to him?

Automatically reacting to his remote manner she said coolly, 'I've managed to do that so far without mishap,' and began to descend the steep staircase carefully with Marcus gazing around, wide eyed.

Once at the bottom she didn't linger for further downbeat comments. As soon as Marcus was strapped into her car's baby seat, she drove the short distance to the nursery. Handing him over reluctantly to the excellent Beth, she then returned to the surgery complex to sort out her calls for the day.

As usual, she found the staff gathered in the kitchen with their mugs of tea, except for Harry who apparently had taken his into his consulting room. Crossly, she hoped he would stay there until she'd set off on her rounds.

He did, and as she drove along the coast road to the shop by the harbour to check on Rory's injured leg once again, she couldn't help thinking how typical it was. The first man she'd had any social contact with in ages had the kind of looks and the background that appealed to her, but clearly he also had a dual personality!

He'd given her the heater of his own free will. It wasn't as if she'd asked him for it. She wanted favours from no one, was her own woman, and intended to stay that way. Nevertheless, it had given her a nice feeling inside to know that he'd tuned into her needs twice in two days.

So hang onto the memory of it, she warned herself. It isn't going to happen again, and if by some strange chance it should, don't go all gooey-eyed, just be pleasant but aloof.

She had to pass a side turning to the Enderbys' farm on her way to the harbour and stopped off to enquire how Pamela was progressing.

George was there by himself again and informed her that his daughter-in-law had come through the surgery, and had been taken to the high-dependency unit.

'It was a miracle the way you and Harry Balfour saved her life,' the old man said huskily. 'We are fortunate to have him with us again as I'm told that he was doing greater things in Australia than running a village practice.

'But his Aunt Barbara is a great one for getting people to do what she wants and it was she that persuaded him to come home. Though I don't think he needed much coaxing after what happened to him out there. That Cassie was a fiery madam, but it seems as if she took on more than she could handle when she tried to overtake a big truck without warning.

'It's a pity he didn't come back to us in the spring when the bluebells out in their glory, the skies so blue and the sea a joy to behold, instead of on a grey day in January.'

'It won't be long before that happens,' she consoled. 'This month is almost out, then February is the shortest one on the calendar, and when it is gone, Easter won't be far away.' Feeling that she needed to be on her way, and reeling slightly from discovering the awful manner in which Harry's wife had died, she said goodbye to George and drove off in the direction of the fishing-tackle shop.

Rory's leg was definitely on the mend and when she'd changed the dressing once more, Jake said, 'We're going to see his Mum and Dad this afternoon. Knowing that the leg is clear of the infection will be one thing less for them to worry about, thanks to you, Nurse.'

'I'm just doing my job.' she told him as she prepared to leave uncle and nephew to their own devices. Then, given his reaction of the previous day to discovering she was a single mum, she was surprised when Jake said, 'We're going out in the boat on Saturday and the invitation is still there if you can manage to come.'

'What sort is it?' she asked warily. 'Has it got a cabin?'

'Yes, of course,' was the reply. 'It's not the *Queen Mary* but she's a nice little craft.'

'I'll think about it,' she told him to avoid refusing outright. Sailing on the open sea in the middle of winter with Marcus was not something she was going to con-template. Maybe if the invitation was still there in the spring, but not now. Although, if she was honest, she couldn't see herself ever considering going sailing with

Jake—she just wasn't that interested in spending more time with him, however nice he was.

As the day took its course, the man on her mind was not the amiable Jake. It was the cool reception she'd received earlier from a more mature member of the opposite sex that kept intruding into her thoughts.

Had he thought when she'd wished him a friendly good morning up on the landing that his concern on the night before had encouraged her to be over-familiar? She shuddered at the thought. From now on she would be so distant he might want his heater back to cope with the drop in temperature.

Harry had watched her from the window of his consulting room as she'd driven off, clearly offended, and told himself he was crazy. He was the one who'd crossed the divide between stranger and acquaintance. It hadn't been Phoebe who'd made the gestures that he was now halfway to regretting, but neither did he have to upset her by trying to re-establish a sense of distance between them.

Then he reminded himself that he wouldn't have been able to sleep easily with a crying baby so close, and it had been the same with the heater. It was essential that in January's chill mother and child should be warm. Perhaps he should simply embrace being neighbourly?

Sighing, he called in his first patient and let the day ahead take hold of him. Maybe when they were both in their apartments tonight, he would get the chance to make amends. Until then the surgery was full of the coughs and sneezes that spread diseases, along with a few patients with more serious illnesses to keep him on his toes.

One of them was in charge of the information centre on the coast road just above the beach. She'd recently had shingles, which hadn't all come to the surface as they should have. Now the stabbing pains of the illness had flared up again quite seriously and she was in a lot of discomfort.

'Shingles, or herpes zoster, is an odd illness,' he told her. 'For some people it's straightforward. The red rash appears, usually on the upper half of the body, then turns to blisters, and because it is connected with the nerve ends it can be very painful, but once the blisters have gone it usually settles down.

'Though not always. For some the pain is there in the background for a long time, especially as in your case, where the rash didn't all come out. Sometimes other medication that the patient is taking can bring back the pain in those areas. I see that you've recently been prescribed a steroid-based inhaler for asthma. It is possible that the steroids could be the reason for the return of the pain.

'So we will try taking you off that kind of inhaler and put you on one that doesn't contain them. It won't be as effective with regard to the asthma, I'm afraid, so I'll need to keep a close eye on you, but let's see if no longer being involved with steroids reduces the pain.'

When he'd made out the prescription and she was ready to go, the patient asked, 'How are you enjoying being back in Bluebell Cove, Dr Balfour?'

'It's good,' he told her, realising it was the truth. 'It feels strange, of course. I've been gone five years, but there's a sort of agelessness about this place that calms the spirit if you let it.'

When Phoebe arrived back at the practice he was still seeing patients from the late surgery and once she'd updated the notes of those she'd visited, she drove to the nursery to collect Marcus.

He greeted her as he usually did with a wide smile and arms outstretched, and what Harry had said about starting a family came back to her. When it came to the crunch she hadn't thought twice about it, but it was a fact that she was all her little one had to care for him. There was no one else in his life for him to love and if anything happened to her... Banishing the upsetting train of thought from her mind, she was cross with Harry for putting it in her head in the first place.

As she carried Marcus up to the apartments Phoebe was grateful that they had their own entrance. It meant that her comings and goings were not on view to surgery staff—most especially her unpredictable neighbour.

After being given the cold shoulder that morning, she was in no rush to meet him again. In a moment of rebellion she decided that once Marcus was tucked up for the night, she was going to give the decorating a miss and spend a quiet evening in front of the television with a bottle of wine and a box of chocolate. And she just might get dressed up for it as well, even though there would only be herself to see the result!

* * *

When surgery was over Harry didn't go straight up to the apartment. He wanted to make things right with his neighbour, but not to go butting in while she and the baby were having their evening meal or while she was bathing him.

So, not yet having tried the culinary delights on offer in Bluebell Cove, he went for a meal in a restaurant on the coast road where the food was wholesome and delicious and included some of his favourite Devonshire dishes.

When he'd finished what he felt was the best meal he'd had in months, he stopped off once again at Four Winds House on the headland as a follow-up to what Ethan had told him about his uncle's prostate problems.

Keith needed another check up, which would allow Harry to decide whether action was required. A quiet word to his uncle as he was leaving would be a spur to sort out an appointment at the hospital and ensure that Barbara wasn't worried by this news of her husband's health when she was already so busy struggling with her own.

He didn't know if his cousin Jenna knew about her father's problem and was going to sound her out at the first opportunity. She'd been a practice nurse at the surgery until little Lily's birth, and now her only connection with health care was as her husband's receptionist when he saw private patients at the clinic he ran from home.

The older folk were delighted to see him and Barbara's first comment was about the surgery and how was he settling in.

'Fine,' he told her. 'It's good to be back. The days are

lengthening and I'm looking forward to when it's going to be warm enough to swim in the sea.'

'Do you see much of Phoebe and young Marcus in the other apartment?' Keith asked, unknowingly bringing to mind where his last call of the day was going to be.

'We're in contact in the surgery, of course, during her comings and goings,' he replied, 'but that's it. We've met a couple of times upstairs but only briefly. We try not to disturb each other after working hours if we can.' And if that wasn't a distortion of the truth he didn't know what was!

When he was ready to go, Keith came to the door with him as he'd expected, and Harry said in a low voice, 'Ethan has passed on to me your concerns about your rising prostate count, and I feel that it is time you had another check-up at the hospital. Is it all right with you if I make an appointment?'

'Yes, of course,' was the reply, 'but I don't want Barbara to know about it. Time to tell her when, or if, there is something to tell.'

'And Jenna?'

'The same applies there. My daughter is having one of the happiest times of her life with a new husband and daughter that she adores. I don't want to be the one who bursts the bubble if I can help it.'

'She won't like it that you've kept it from her,' he warned.

'It's as I've just said, it will be time to tell when there's something that needs telling.'

The wine and the added warmth in the room were making Phoebe feel drowsy and relaxed for the first time in ages, but when she heard the tap on her door she was jolted out of it.

Surely it wasn't Harry, she thought through the warm haze that had settled on her, not after this morning. Yet he was the only other person who had a key for the entrance to the apartments.

With a half-full wine glass in her hand she glided across to the door and opened it with a sort of queenly grace. Sure enough, he was there, eyes widening in amazement at the vision before him. She was dressed in a long black skirt, a white sequined top and wearing more make-up than he'd ever seen her use before.

'Yes?' she said with the regal mode still on her. If he hadn't been so taken aback he would have laughed.

He could hear a voice in the background and thought, Oh, God! She's got company. I'm going to look a right fool.

'I just want to say I'm sorry if I was rather abrupt this morning. That's it really,' he explained in a low voice.

'Don't give it another thought,' she said smoothly, as if she hadn't been smarting for most of the day. 'Do sleep well.' As he turned to go, she shut the door and went back to what she'd been doing, which wasn't a lot with only the television for company.

So Phoebe of the pale beauty and long brown hair was not the lonely single mother he'd assumed her to be, Harry thought as he cringed from the embarrassment of the last few moments. She'd been entertaining someone all dressed up and waving a wine glass in front of him to make sure he got the message.

So what? Surely he wasn't bothered about that, was he? He was the guy who was wearing a mental badge that said, *Touch me not*. He wasn't going to start yearning after the district nurse! She was the exact opposite of what Cassie had been like, though what was wrong with that?

He poured himself a beer, watched television for a while then went to bed, but not to sleep. His ears were straining for the sound of Phoebe's visitor departing, but it never came. He finally fell asleep just as dawn was breaking.

To his surprise, she had already dropped Marcus off at the nursery and, looking poised for action, was sorting out her home visits when he came downstairs the next morning.

On observing her, his first thought was that she didn't look like someone on the morning after a night of passion. But it had definitely been a man's voice he'd heard coming from her sitting room when she'd opened the door to him and listened graciously while he'd humbled himself outside on the landing.

Whoever it was, she'd certainly dressed up for him, he thought with sudden envy. At that moment she turned, saw him observing her, and said politely, 'Good morning, Dr Balfour.'

'Good morning,' he replied heavily, and went into his consulting room, before coming out again and asking as if some unseen force was putting the words into his mouth, 'Did you have a nice evening with your friend?'

He watched her blink in surprise. 'I'm not quite sure what you mean,' she told him coolly, 'unless you're referring to last night, and you have been jumping to conclusions if you are. I spent the evening alone. What you saw when I opened the door was just me, trying to have a pleasant evening with a bottle of wine and the television.'

Harry felt his jaw go slack as what she was saying registered. Phoebe wasn't wrong about him jumping to conclusions. It was just one more instance of him interfering in her affairs. Yet there was a feeling of relief inside him as well as mortification as he admitted to himself that he hadn't wanted her to be with some other guy all dressed up and drinking wine.

He groaned. 'I am so sorry. If I promise faithfully to mind my own business in future, will you forgive me?'

She wanted to tell him she could forgive him for much more than that.

Despite their recent misunderstandings, he was still the first person who had treated her as a normal woman, with her own needs and reassurances, since she'd had Marcus. The phrase 'single mother' had a kind of stigma to it, as if she'd committed some sort of crime, but he didn't make her feel like that.

She smiled and he thought again how strangely beautiful she was. 'Of course I can forgive you,' she said softly, 'There is no reason why we can't be friends, is there, having found ourselves living in such close proximity?'

'No, none at all,' he replied steadily, as if it was going

to be easy to be just that and nothing else. Then, as Millie went to open the doors to let in the sick and suffering at half past eight, they separated, each to their own functions.

The following day was Saturday and Phoebe intended doing what she usually did at the weekend—going into town to shop. She'd rung Jake to tell him she wouldn't be going sailing with him and Rory, and he hadn't seemed too disappointed, which had been a cause for relief.

She couldn't help but compare Jake with Harry, who, though he had some odd ideas about bringing children into the world, had nevertheless been there for her in the middle of the night, ready and willing to assist her in any way that he could.

It was amazing that someone without, or even with, family ties hadn't made a play for him already. His attractions were many—tall, broad shouldered, with a direct hazel gaze and dark russet thatch of hair to complete the picture.

Yet she'd observed there was a downside to him. He could display an abrupt kind of reserve that spoke of a life she knew nothing about, a life that had contained loneliness and neglect when he'd had no one to turn to for comfort.

All right, she'd had her own pit of despair to climb out of, but from that had come Marcus and everything had suddenly seemed worthwhile. What had happened to Harry to make him so unhappy?

She wondered what his wife had been like. Obviously someone special for him to be ready to leave the beautiful countryside and coastlines of Devon to move to her country. Had he ever thought then that one day he would return without her?

CHAPTER FOUR

PHOEBE was used to the noise and bustle of the town. It was like any other Saturday morning. She was wandering around the excellent outdoor market with Marcus in his baby buggy, gazing around him with interest, when she heard her name called. Turning, she saw Jake and Rory loaded down with shopping.

'I thought you were going sailing,' she said with a smile for her young patient.

'We are,' Jake told her. 'We've just come to get provisions for the weekend and are wondering who else we're going to see from the surgery.'

'Why?'

'We've just seen the doctor that you called out to look at Rory's leg.' She observed him in surprise. 'You know, the new guy.'

'You mean Dr Balfour. Where was he?' she enquired, not sure if she wanted to see Harry again so soon after their conversation the previous day.

'He was coming out of Hunter's Hill Hospital as we drove past.'

'Ah, I see.'

She didn't really, but had no wish to discuss the

comings and goings of her neighbour with Jake and Rory. Yet she was curious to know why Harry had been visiting the hospital.

But she'd come to do some food shopping and as they went on their way she gave her attention to free-range eggs, farm-cured bacon and fresh vegetables, with Marcus looking on.

That was followed by a saunter around a department store and on impulse she bought a pretty sweater and some well-cut jeans, then took Marcus for lunch in the bistro there.

It was as she was making her way back to the car park, pushing the buggy with one hand and carrying what wouldn't fit underneath it with the other, when a voice called from behind, 'Hang on a moment, Phoebe. Let me give you a lift.' And the man who never seemed to be out of her thoughts was by her side in an instant.

'Are y-you all r-right?' she stammered, overcome by nerves at his sudden proximity.

'Yes, of course. Why do you ask?' he wanted to know.

'I met up with Jake and Rory and they'd seen you coming out of Hunter's Hill.'

'Are you referring to the lad with the injured leg and that uncle of his?' he questioned.

'Er, yes.'

'So are you always on such friendly terms with your patients?'

'Not always. It's just that they wanted me to go sailing with them this weekend, but needless to say I refused. I wouldn't take Marcus on that sort of a jaunt in this kind of weather.'

'I'm glad to hear it,' he commented dryly, 'and as to why I was at Hunter's Hill, I'd come into town to shop and thought I'd pop in to see how Pamela Enderby is progressing. Apart from the fact that you and I saved her life, she and I were at school together. I *have* got a past in these parts, you know.'

'Yes, I do, which is more than I have. My past is all wrapped up in the thirst for success and a lack of interest in the things of life that really matter.'

He was observing her thoughtfully. 'And are you going to tell me about how it all went wrong some time?'

'No,' she said flatly. 'It isn't worth telling. So, can we get back to Pamela?'

He nodded. 'According to the registrar I spoke to, she should be home soon. The operation was a success. So it will be up to the neurosurgeon to decide what the hospital does as a follow-up to the nightmare that we walked into that day.

'It was strange, how we barely knew each other, yet in those desperate moments when we worked on her it was as if we were welded into one.'

She nodded. What Harry had just said described exactly how she'd felt.

There'd been an unexpected affinity and it was still there, a closeness that she was uncomfortable about. Although he seemed to be continually at her elbow, she had a feeling that he too had his doubts about it. Another odd thing was that out of all the surgery staff, apart from

Leo, who hadn't been there long, she was the only one Harry hadn't known previously.

At the time he'd left to go to Australia she'd been living in London with Darren as a new bride with not a cloud in her sky. No doubt Harry had been feeling the same, having met the woman of his dreams, but they'd both been brought down to earth since then. And now, as he strode alongside her, carrying the shopping, it felt just as right as it had when they'd resuscitated Pamela Enderby.

As the car park came into sight she put her daydreams to one side and came back to realities by commenting, 'I can't see your car and it isn't one that's easily missed.'

Beside his bright red convertible, her own small runabout felt totally insignificant, but it sufficed for what she wanted it for and that was all that mattered.

'It isn't there,' Harry explained. 'I walked here.' She observed him in surprise. 'Yes, it was a long walk, but I wanted to see some of the places again that once were so familiar. Also, I needed the exercise but now that I've had it, I wouldn't say no to a lift back to the village!'

'Yes, of course,' she agreed. 'Once Marcus is strapped in safely and I've put my shopping in the boot, we'll be off.'

'I'll see to him while you stash the shopping,' he said, and she thought that the offer was a definite improvement on the other night, when he'd held him stiffly in his arms and she'd told him laughingly that Marcus wouldn't bite.

She wasn't to know that Harry wanted to see if the feel of that small warm body against his was as satisfying and wholesome as it had been that first time. As he lifted him out of the buggy Marcus had a smile for him and Harry said, 'He's a happy little guy, isn't he, all considering?'

Phoebe was putting the shopping into the boot of the car and she raised her head sharply. 'Considering? Considering what? That he hasn't got a father?'

'Well, yes.'

'Quality is better than quantity any time. He won't ever feel lonely and lost while I'm around.' And she closed the boot with a resounding slam as if to empha- sise the fierce statement..

'That I can well believe,' he said with a smile that took the edge off her irritation. He bent to fasten the harness of the car seat around the baby and then slid into the passenger seat beside her and they were off.

They were silent for most of the journey, but it was clear Phoebe hadn't forgotten what he'd said. As the village came into view, she continued their earlier con- versation. 'I suppose your comments earlier were also raising the question of how happy Marcus would be if anything happened to me, and if he was left all alone in the world. That might be a fair comment but, Harry, everything we do in life is a risk. To me, a bigger risk would have been to let Marcus be saddled with a father who didn't want him. I think you might have been down a similar road to that so will understand what I mean.'

When she looked across at him his expression was sombre but he didn't say anything. She wondered if his hurt went too deep to talk about it to someone he'd only just met.

* * *

They were back at the surgery and as Harry was lifting Marcus out of the car, he suddenly said, 'Thanks for the lift, Phoebe. In return, I'll cook dinner tonight if you like.'

Oh, yes, she would 'like' was her immediate reaction to the suggestion, but like many travellers on the sea of life they both had baggage. On her part a hurtful divorce that had not been about infidelity but about rejection and selfishness, and on his a recent bereavement that so far he hadn't spoken of.

So was she going to accept the offer because attached to it was going to be some prime time with him? No, she wasn't. It would be crazy to step any further into each other's lives than they had done already.

She let him down gently. 'No, thanks just the same. I've got our meal already organised for tonight,' and with a final turn of the screw, 'I'll see you on Monday, Harry.' Ashamed that she hadn't had the nerve to tell him the truth—that the more she saw of him, the more time she wanted them to spend together—she took Marcus from him and slowly climbed the stairs to what was left of another lonely weekend.

He was pushing his luck with Phoebe, Harry thought as he followed her some seconds later. Why couldn't he have been satisfied with meeting her in the town and being near her in the car during the lift home? Oh, no, he'd wanted more, and ought to know better.

When he'd left Australia, he'd just been beginning to get over the horror of the accident that had cost Cassie her life. He'd set off for home deciding that those who stay alone are less likely to get hurt, so what was he doing now? Hanging around the first woman he'd come into close contact with like a teenage Romeo, that was what.

If he didn't back off, Phoebe was going to start feeling trapped up there with him continually butting into her life, and there was really only one answer to that. He had to do what he'd intended on coming back to Bluebell Cove—find a permanent place to live.

He had expected his house hunting to be a leisurely thing, with the apartment a base from which to view in his own good time. properties that were on offer. But then again, he hadn't expected to be living in such closeness to a single mother whose solitariness was pulling at his heart strings.

So why not start house hunting today? he thought bleakly. There wasn't anything to stop him. He was sure that Phoebe wouldn't be sorry to see him go.

The village's estate agent was open but doing little business because of the time of year, so the young guy behind the counter had all the time in the world to tell him about an impressive list of properties for sale. That would be much reduced in quantity and greatly increased in price during the summer months.

There was an attractively converted barn, a large period cottage down a wooded lane not far from the village centre, a luxurious apartment in a new complex on the coast road, and even a small manor house that he could probably afford if he pulled out all the stops, but he couldn't see himself rattling around a place like that on his own.

As the estate agent expounded upon their delights and advantages, he found he couldn't work up enthusiasm for any of them because he was seeing a flight of worn uncarpeted stairs, a landing with two old oak doors on it, and behind one of them was...what?

A mother and child that he couldn't stop thinking about, and they were making his longing for solitude go to pot. That was why the brochures of the properties displayed in front of him were not gripping his imagination.

Yet maybe if he viewed a couple of them he might become interested, and if he wasn't there would still be plenty of others to consider. So he made a lukewarm appointment to view the manor house and the converted barn on Sunday morning.

'Guess what I saw when I was out walking my dog yesterday,' Lucy, the senior practice nurse, said first thing on Monday morning, when all the staff—with the exception of Harry—were warming up in the kitchen as usual.

Phoebe had just arrived after depositing Marcus at the nursery and joined in the laughter when Leo suggested jokingly, 'Naturists on the beach?'

'No,' she replied in hushed tones. 'I saw Howard from the estate agent's showing our leader around one of the nicest houses in the area, Glades Manor!'

'Wow!' Leo said, and Phoebe thought miserably wow indeed. So much for their short, thought-provoking acquaintance in the apartments above. She would still see Harry in the surgery, but if he moved out there would no longer be the comforting feeling of having him near when their day's work was done.

Yet she thought she understood his reasoning. Despite his initial awkwardness, he'd been great with her and Marcus. Most likely because he'd found himself in such close proximity and had felt that being neighbourly was the least he could do, but Harry had his own life to lead, as she did. It stood to sense that he wasn't going to want to be living in an average apartment for long if he had the means to purchase something as prestigious as Glades Manor, which stood in several acres among the green meadows of the Devonshire countryside.

Leaving the staff still chatting about the comings and goings of Ethan Lomax's successor, she went into Reception where the list of calls she had to make would be waiting for her. There she found the man on her mind leaning on the counter and chatting to Millie.

Harry was observing her keenly as she approached and deciding that Phoebe wasn't well or something had upset her. Unaware of what was being talked about in the kitchen at the end of the passage, he hoped it wasn't anything to do with him.

'Are you okay?' he asked in a low voice as the phone rang at that moment and Millie was occupied.

'Yes, I'm fine,' she lied. 'I'm just about to sort out my day and then I'm off. Rory doesn't need me any more, but George Enderby's leg needs watching and my patient with the insulin injections is still not feeling too confident about giving them to himself.

'Then there is old Jeremy Davenport, who has developed a bed sore after being confined to bed for so long in hospital with a difficult leg fracture. He's home now but still incapacitated and the bed sore hasn't completely gone, so it's been passed to me.'

He was nodding gravely. 'That sounds enough to keep you occupied but, Phoebe, if you get the chance, take note of snowdrops in cottage gardens. The daffodils and crocus won't be long either. They are some of the things I missed while down under, as well as women with pale unblemished skin that the sun hasn't tanned. It was the first thing I noticed about you.'

Was he paying her a compliment or hinting that she looked wishy-washy? she wondered, and in the next moment thought she had the answer as he went on to say dryly, 'Just as long as you're not anaemic.'

She was picking up her bag and about to head for the door. 'I'm not. My mother's skin was the same.'

'And where is *she* now?'

'She died shortly after I was married. We lost my father when I was small. Luckily my sister and her husband filled the gap when my marriage broke up. Katie and Rob were there for me every step of the way, and it made all the difference. Rejection slowly turned into revival.' As the rest of the staff came filing in from the kitchen, Phoebe wished she hadn't opened up to him about her past so much, and said briskly, 'I'm off, Dr Balfour, and I won't forget about the snowdrops.'

I won't forget that you are house hunting either, she thought glumly as she left the village behind and drove along the coast road to the first of her home visits.

Was it significant that it had happened the morning after she'd been so unapproachable and turned down his offer of dinner? she pondered. Yet surely he hadn't set such store by her acceptance of the offer that he'd decided to move into somewhere more permanent when she'd refused.

One thing was sure, there was no way she was going to mention Glades Manor to Harry. He had no idea that Lucy had seen him viewing it when she'd been out walking her dog, and she felt he would take a dim view of it being surgery gossip that could end up on the village grapevine. If he didn't tell her she wasn't going to ask. It was as simple as that.

As the days went by, the house remained on the market and Harry and Phoebe were polite but distant when they met on the wooden staircase or on the landing.

He didn't knock on her door again as January shivered into February, and, as he'd reminded her they would, daffodils were nodding in golden perfection in small gardens and sheltered glades, with crocus blooming beside them less gracefully but just as beautiful.

Harry *had* been impressed by the small manor house, it had been beautifully restored by the present owner, but every time he thought about it, he felt that it was a house that needed a family. It needed parents with growing children and maybe more to come, not a wifeless, childless, empty vessel like him.

He was staying clear of Phoebe as much as possible in the evenings and at weekends because he felt that he'd been too pushy. Deep down, he knew that finding a permanent place to live *was* the thing to do, but something was holding him back. As he lay sleepless, or at the best tossed and turned restlessly in his solitary bed, the reason why was just a few feet away behind a door that remained steadfastly closed against him.

Phoebe had no intention of attending the Valentine's Day ball that the village's social events committee was organising, until Lucy surprised her by offering to look after Marcus while she went.

'It's time you got out and about more,' she said kindly, 'and if you could bring baby Marcus across to Jenna and Lucas's house, where I've promised to babysit Lily, I can look after them both. So what do you think?' As Phoebe hesitated, she continued, 'There will be a few there from the surgery. Even Harry has bought a ticket, though I doubt he'll make use of it.'

'Yes, all right then,' Phoebe said. 'I'd love to go. Marcus is always asleep by seven o'clock at the latest, so when its time to go I can carry him across wrapped in a warm blanket and settle him on the couch for the evening. Once he's in a really deep sleep he rarely wakes up so you shouldn't have any problems with him.'

When Harry heard Lucy telling Maria, the other practice nurse, that she was going to mind Lily and Marcus on the night of the ball, he stopped Phoebe one morning as she was leaving the practice and wanted to know why she hadn't asked him to take care of Marcus.

He said, 'It seems to me that you're making heavy weather of something that could be so simple if you left me in charge of him.'

'I was told that you've already bought a ticket,' she said, trying to conceal her surprise at his suggestion.

'Yes, I have, but it doesn't say I'll be going, unless you're short of an escort.'

'Do you have to make me sound so needy?' she snapped, irritated.

'I'm not. I just thought you might be going with that Jake person.'

'What?' she cried with increasing indignation. 'Why him?'

'Thought he had the hots for you, that's all.'

'He might have had, but they soon cooled down when he found out about Marcus, and before you ask if I was upset, the answer is no.'

'So you'll let *me* take you to this Valentine's Ball, then?'

'If you intend on going, yes.' Still rattled by him taking her for granted, she went on, 'It will be one step better than standing around the edges of the dance floor like a wallflower.'

Harry was taking in the sarcasm and trying not to smile. He hadn't *intended* doing anything of the sort until he'd discovered that she would be there, but now he was totally tuned in to the thought of dancing the night away with her in his arms.

She went out on the district then, still stunned by his offer to mind Marcus while she went to the ball but glad that Lucy's offer had come first. For the first time she was now looking forward to it, though she had no intention of letting Harry know that. Instead, like most women with a special occasion in view, she was already debating what to wear.

Since splitting up with Darren, the only clothes she'd bought had been maternity wear, plus those in the department store on the Saturday when Harry had seen her on the way to the car park. Unless she could find time for another quick trip in to town before the ball, it would have to be one of the smart outfits she'd worn when she'd been married, which belonged to what she thought of as the days of wine and poses.

There was a new patient on her list that morning. The surgery had sent her to evaluate what kind of care and assistance was needed by the local plumber, who had just been unexpectedly diagnosed with a form of inoperable stomach cancer that was terminal.

Expecting to see a very sick man, she was amazed to see him painting the outside of his bungalow on one of the lanes leading from the village's main street with every appearance of good health. When he assured her that he was fine, she left him to it, knowing that soon he was going to need the special care of a hospice, but for now she was content to leave him to enjoy a task that he might not be able to do for much longer.

Back at the surgery Harry was too busy to think any further about the strange conversation they'd just had, or the outcome of it. It was one of those mornings when one crisis was following another.

The first was parents bringing in their seriously unwell five-year-old daughter. The moment he saw the child Harry realised that she was showing signs of meningitis—the light was hurting her eyes, she was running a temperature, had an inflamed throat and, most worrying of all, the red rash of the illness that was one of its most easy to recognise symptoms.

He was amazed that they hadn't taken their child straight to hospital, yet was aware that where most parents were swift to panic, others were slow to grasp the seriousness of a situation. Within seconds he was phoning for an ambulance and emphasising the extreme seriousness of the little girl's condition.

The response to his call was fast and soon she was on her way to hospital with sirens screeching and paramedics and her stunned parents watching over her.

As he'd watched them go he had prayed they would get there before the infection took its terrible toll. If the child was treated quickly there would be a chance, but modern medicines and the Almighty would be equally responsible for the outcome.

The next person to give grave cause for concern was Lorraine Forrest, who controlled the school crossing as lollipop lady. A pleasant thirty-year-old with twin boys in the juniors section, she'd been knocked down outside the surgery while doing her job by a car driver who had collapsed at the wheel. A member of the public had come rushing inside to inform the doctors.

Harry and Leo were out and running in a flash to find the young mother lying on the crossing with a crowd beginning to gather around her and the local policeman frantically redirecting the traffic.

The driver was still slumped over the wheel and passersby had just managed to get the car door open when the two doctors appeared, so Leo went to check him out while Harry knelt beside Lorraine.

She was semi-conscious, with one of her legs bent awkwardly beneath her and bleeding from the temple where she must have hit the road or come into contact with the car bonnet.

When he checked her heartbeat it was erratic, which was not surprising under the circumstances, and she was beginning to go into shock. She was cold and shaking as if with ague and needed warmth to help ward off the effects. For goodness' sake, where were Lucy and Maria, the practice nurses?

'Has anyone sent for an ambulance?' he bellowed above the noise of the traffic and the voices all around him.

'Yes, I've asked for two,' the policeman said, pausing in his task for a moment.

This is hellish, Harry thought. Where *were* the rest of his staff? He couldn't leave the injured woman but she desperately needed blankets over her and any other kind of heating they could rustle up in the surgery.

He was about to tell one of the onlookers to go and find a nurse when Phoebe's small runabout pulled up at the kerb beside him. Thank God, he thought to himself.

She was out of the car in a second and he cried, 'Blankets and anything else you can find to keep her warm. Lorraine is in shock and we can't move her because she has what looks like a serious leg fracture.'

She turned and was gone, returning seconds later with a pile of blankets and a hot-water bottle that she'd found. As they did their best to wrap the blankets around the injured woman and placed the hot-water bottle at her feet, he gave a tight smile and said, 'Is it history repeating itself, do you think?'

She smiled back. 'It might be. If you are wondering what's happened to Lucy and Maria, Lorraine's mother was in the waiting room and she collapsed when someone came in with the news that her daughter had been hit by a car. She's only just coming round because she banged her head on a radiator as she fell.'

He groaned. 'What a mess! Leo is doing his stuff with the old guy who caused all this. We don't know yet what made him collapse at the wheel but as soon as the ambulances arrive, our two casualties—or perhaps I should say three, including Lorraine's mother—need to be taken to A and E fast.'

Leo came across at that moment and informed them, 'The guy who is responsible for all this appears to have had a heart attack. He's alive and is conscious now, but there would have been nothing he could have done to avoid the accident. He's still in the car. I thought he would be warmer there.' Without waiting for any comments from the senior partner and the district nurse, he hurried back to his patient.

'How do you come to be here, Phoebe?' Harry asked as the church clock struck twelve.

'I came to get something to eat as lunchtime was drawing near and found myself in the middle of this. Do we know who the man in the car is?'

'Yes. I heard someone in the crowd say he's an artist who has only recently moved into Bluebell Cove. His name is Adrian Docherty and he has a history of cardiac problems.'

He was checking Lorraine's heartbeat and pulse again, observing her anxiously. He commented, 'I hope they keep the children inside until the ambulances have been. It would be dreadful if her boys should see their mother like this.'

'Charlotte Templeton is headmistress and she's no fool,' she told him.

'They'll be having their school dinners at the moment and probably be kept inside the big hall afterwards until this catastrophe is sorted.'

She was tucking the blankets more closely around the injured woman and said quietly, with her head bent to the task, 'I dread that one day something like this might happen to me, because apart from Katie and Rob I'm the only family that Marcus has got.'

'There's his father surely.'

'He has forfeited the right to be called that.'

'That sounds a bit strong.'

'Not without just cause.'

'So do you want to tell me about it when we have our three casualties safely on the way to A and E?'

She shook her head. 'No, I don't think so, Harry. Just as you wouldn't want to talk about losing your wife.'

Or would he? she thought when she saw his expression. Having introduced an awkward moment, Phoebe wished she hadn't. Thankfully the emergency services arrived at that moment and all else was put to one side.

CHAPTER FIVE

IT WAS early afternoon and the surgery was back to its normal well-organised routine after the distressing events of the morning. Phoebe had gone to carry out the rest of her house calls and the two doctors were having a quick bite before setting out on *their* home visits, which were going to be much later than usual due to the accident on the crossing.

As Harry drove along the coast road to answer a request for a visit from the husband of a patient with dementia, he was intending to stop off at his aunt and uncle's house on the way back. The results had come through from the hospital for the prostate check-up he'd arranged for Keith and he wanted to pass them on to him as soon as possible.

The day had started on a high, he was thinking, with the promise of taking Phoebe to the Valentine's Ball, but before he'd had the chance to feel any pleasure at the prospect there had been a series of lows. His thoughts went out to the three people whose lives had come unstuck in the surgery area in a matter of minutes.

Thankfully, what he had to tell Keith was not in the same category. The tests had shown that his prostate count hadn't risen any more. It had steadied and for the present there was no cause for alarm. But he would have to pass on the good news in private as Barbara hadn't known that there *was* a problem, so the least said to her the better.

But first he had to see what was wrong at a big detached house overlooking the sea, where the sadness and frustration of dementia ruled the lives of its two occupants.

'Harry!' Peter Drummond exclaimed as the two men shook hands.

'I didn't know you were back with us until I rang the surgery this morning. Deborah and I seem to live such isolated lives these days. We rarely get to the village, or anywhere else for that matter.'

'She gets frightened if I want to take her anywhere and only feels safe inside the house, so that is where we spend most of our days. It's hard to believe that she was once the life and soul of every party, but that's how it is.'

The Drummonds had been newly retired from the hotel business when Harry had left Bluebell Cove and they'd been at the centre of every social event for miles around before that. It was only after he'd gone that Deborah had begun to show signs of the deterioration that came with the illness.

'So what's the problem?' he asked as Peter showed him into a large sitting room overlooking the sea, where just as immaculate as she'd always been, his wife was staring into space.

'A chest infection of some sort.' he replied. 'Deborah

has been coughing most of the night and her breathing isn't good.'

Harry sounded her chest and coaxed her to let him look down her throat, and when he'd finished he said, 'You are right about that. I'll drop a prescription off at the chemist and arrange for it to be delivered to you, Peter. What about the flu jab? Has Deborah had that... and the once-only pneumonia injection?'

He nodded. 'Yes. Phoebe, the district nurse, has given her them both.'

'That's good then, and make sure that Deborah takes the full dose of the antibiotics I've prescribed, won't you, Peter?'

As he was on the point of leaving he asked, 'How often does the district nurse visit?'

'Three times a week. She helps with Deborah's bathing, offers feeding suggestions and is generally most helpful. Although my wife doesn't know who she is from one week to the next, she is always more tranquil when Phoebe has been.'

When he arrived back at the practice, after bringing light into his uncle's life when he'd gone to the door with him to say goodbye, there was news from the hospital regarding the casualties of the morning.

Lorraine was conscious and was waiting for them to operate on her knee, where some of the bones were shattered and would need pinning together. Her husband had been informed about the accident and had taken the children out of school so that they could all be together, and the family was now waiting for her to be taken to theatre.

Her mother was being kept in overnight, but was due to be discharged in the morning, and the artist—the unintentional cause of the disastrous events—was in Coronary Care, where he was in a serious condition.

Phoebe had arrived as Lucy was in the middle of regaling Harry with the bulletin from the hospital. Although he thought she looked cold and tired, she had a smile for him and he had to look away and grip the corner of the desk that he was perched on to control the wave of longing that washed over him.

When he looked up she was gone again, this time to collect Marcus from the nursery, and she hadn't come back by the time he was ready to ascend the wooden staircase at the end of his working day, which was strange.

It was half past six, two hours since she'd gone to pick Marcus up, and he was watching the fingers of the clock like someone hypnotised. Surely nothing else could go wrong, he thought desperately. But she and her little one were out there somewhere in the dark February night and he was pacing around his apartment like an anxious expectant father, a role that he'd never visualised playing.

When he heard her car pull up on the forecourt down below, his relief was swamped by annoyance and he went down the stairs two at a time. 'Where the dickens have you been?' he cried. 'I've imagined all sorts of things having happened to you!'

She was bending inside the car, undoing the straps

on the baby seat, and as she stretched up with Marcus in her arms she said mildly, as if dealing with a fractious child, 'I've been shopping,' making him feel even more frazzled.

'Shopping! What on earth for, after working all day? Surely nothing could have been that important. And what about this little guy's meal? He looks happy enough, but he must be starving.'

Suddenly her calm deserted her. 'I've been shopping for something to wear on Friday night so that I won't show you up,' she said hotly, and as he observed her in mute astonishment she continued, 'So will you please stop shouting so loudly that the whole village can hear you.'

Turning her back on him, she began to march up the stairs with a parting shot over her shoulder to the effect that she and Marcus had already eaten in a little bistro, and all he was going to need was his bedtime bottle.

'I'm sorry,' he said stiffly as he followed her up. 'If you had just said what you intended doing, I wouldn't have been so tensed up.'

'I'm not used to anyone being concerned on our account, except for Ethan when *he* was here,' she said, calming down as he drew level with her. 'Perhaps I ought to have let you know what I had in mind, and as a fitting finale to a dreadful day I didn't find *anything* to wear.'

She was putting her key in the lock with tears threatening. In a second she had the door open and was gone, closing it behind her with a decisive click.

* * *

Would he ever get it right with Phoebe? Harry wondered as he made himself a belated meal. He'd ranted and raved down there on the practice forecourt as if he had the right and in the process had insulted her by presuming that she hadn't put her child's needs first, all because she hadn't told him where she was going.

Of course Phoebe wouldn't let Marcus be hungry while she tried on clothes in some department store. As well as the beautiful mother, he was letting the beautiful child get to him, he thought wryly, remembering his concerns for Marcus when she'd finally put in an appearance, *and* when he'd offered to baby-sit on the night of the ball and been pipped at the post by Lucy's offer.

He should have just been happy to see that no harm had befallen the two of them and left it at that. His face was tender at the thought of her going all that way, at the end of a long and tiring day, to buy something to wear for his sake. Although, if he was to tell her that he didn't care what she wore, that just being with her would be enough, that would probably be the wrong thing to say as well!

Maybe later he would risk another rebuff by doing the thing he'd been trying so hard not to do over past days—knock on her door and try to make amends for his churlishness. But first he had to give her some breathing space, let her see Marcus settled for the night and give her time to unwind before he barged into her life again.

He wasn't to know that Phoebe was fighting the urge to open the door that she'd been so quick to shut in his face and rush across the landing to tell him how sorry she was for causing him so much anxiety, and that she understood his annoyance.

It was true what she'd said about not being used to having anyone so concerned about her, but that didn't mean she'd had to snap at him, especially when it had become clear how worried he'd been.

He was washing up after his scratch meal, with hands deep in warm suds, when he heard her knock. Without drying them, Harry was out of the kitchen, into the hall and opening the door before she had time to change her mind.

She'd changed out of her nurse's uniform and was dressed in the jeans and sweater she'd bought on the day when they'd met up near the open market. Her hair was tied back off her face in a ponytail, and this time, unlike earlier, she'd thrown off her tiredness, wiped away her tears and was about to say her piece.

He stepped back to let her in and as he did so asked, 'Where's Marcus?'

She smiled. 'I would have been disappointed it you hadn't asked, given your recent concern on his behalf. He is asleep in his own little dreamland. I wouldn't have come otherwise.'

He groaned. 'Please don't remind me of my interference. I squirm every time I think about it.'

'You mustn't,' she chided gently. 'It was good of you to care, Harry.' Their glances met. 'I've come to apologise for not telling you that I was going shopping after work. We are such close neighbours it was only fair that I should have let you know.

'My sister and her husband have been the only ones there for me for a long time, so I'm afraid it takes a bit of getting used to when coming from another direction. I have never ever met a man like you before.'

They were only inches away from each other and she could feel a force reaching out between them, a heat that was making her bones melt. She wondered if he could feel it too, yet it didn't seem like it as he was making no attempt to get closer. In fact, it was as if he was rooted to the spot.

But when she reached out and touched his face with gentle fingers, he came alive. In an instant she was in his arms, his mouth was on hers, and the hard strength of his body was telling her without putting it into words how much he wanted her.

But it appeared their magical coming together was not going to go any further. He was loosening his hold and putting her away from him gently as he told her, 'You deserve better than me, Phoebe. I came back to Bluebell Cove intending to steer clear of relationships after losing Cassie. Then I found you almost on my doorstep, and all the vows I'd made to myself were suddenly hard to keep.

'I've always prided myself on my self control but twice this evening I've lost it, the first time in anger, the second in lust, and neither were fair to you. So go back to your child and maybe we can get to know each other all over again at a slower pace.'

So far Phoebe hadn't spoken but now she was finding her voice. It didn't sound like hers because it was cold and clipped, yet it had to be because there was only the two of them there.

'I'm sorry to hear you describe what happened to us a moment ago as lust,' she told him. 'If it had been, we would have been in bed together by now, throwing caution to the wind.

'But you clearly think I might see that as a sign of commitment, and you've just made it clear that you want to keep away from that kind of thing, so fret no further. I was content enough before we met and shall continue to be so without any assistance from you.'

And before he could think of a sensible justification for the further mess he'd just made of everything, she was gone and he made no attempt to follow her.

As Phoebe lay sleepless, the indignation that Harry had aroused in her was disappearing. In the short time that she'd known him she'd grown to care for him, but until now had never realised how much.

She was drawn to his rugged attractiveness and his integrity, and moved at the way he was with Marcus and how he coped with the world of baby care. Those moments in his arms, brief as they had been, had shown her that was where she wanted to be, but if he had his doubts about that kind of closeness, she would have to be patient.

As the fingers of the clock said that it would soon be daylight, she decided that she wouldn't refer again to what had happened between them, that magical moment when, for a few seconds, he'd ignored any reservations he might have and had reached out for her.

She'd known then that he had felt the same heating

of the senses that she had, and the same kind of pull, yet something had made him draw back and she'd been angry and confused. But now all she wanted was to be there for him when he needed her, and maybe one day…

On that thought she turned on her side and slept for what felt like a matter of minutes before Marcus was shaking his cot rails and wanting his breakfast.

Coming down the stairs the next morning, she met Harry returning from an early home visit. When she smiled across at him, she watched his jaw slacken in surprise, but he merely nodded and went to take off his coat in the privacy of his own room, while she began her usual morning routine of driving to the nursery.

Surely Phoebe wasn't going to forgive him for last night's fiasco, he thought as he seated himself behind his desk. He'd been like someone deranged ever since they'd met, behaving totally out of character.

Yet his attraction hadn't exactly been from their *first* meeting. He smiled to himself at the memory of a strange figure peering at him through a crack of the door on his first night in Bluebell Cove.

It had been on the following morning when they'd met officially and he'd seen how beautiful she really was that he'd become entranced. From that moment, he'd gradually come to realise that he wanted Phoebe more than anything he'd ever wanted in his life.

But always there was the downside of his yearning for her—did he want the same things that she wanted, when a happy family for herself and Marcus was at the top of her list?

* * *

The thing uppermost in Phoebe's mind as the week drew to a close was the Valentine's Ball—was Harry still going to take her, and if he was, did she want him to? After all, it was only a few days away, and she still hadn't decided what to wear.

The items of evening wear she'd taken with her when she'd left Darren to his climbing of the ladder of success were all attractive—they'd had to be as the wife of the chairman's protégé. Needless to say, none of them had seen the light of day since, so she supposed there was no harm in giving one of them an airing if she did end up going to the ball.

It was to be held at the Enderbys' luxurious farmhouse, as all special events in Bluebell Cove were, because they had a very large reception room that was just right for those sorts of things. Although Pamela hadn't been home from hospital long after the fall and its consequences, she had insisted that it must still go ahead as the outside caterers that they always used were all geared up to run the whole thing, along with a popular local band.

'I shall just sit at the side and watch,' she'd said to the committee who organised the yearly event, and to her elderly father-in-law George. 'You'll keep me company, won't you, Dad?'

'I will indeed,' he'd replied. 'Neither of us will be getting out our dancing shoes this year, eh, Pammy?'

As one of the members of the events committee, Lucy had been there at the time, and when she'd reported back that conversation, Phoebe had thought that at least Pamela and George had their night mapped out, restricted though it may be. She wished she could say the same for hers.

There'd been little personal contact between Harry and her in the last few days, though they'd been pleasant enough towards each other when they had met. But Phoebe felt like it was the lull before a storm and kept putting off the moment of clearing the air regarding the ball.

If he was going to back out, she was quite prepared to go on her own, but if he didn't say something soon, it was too bad, because she wasn't going to bring up the subject.

'So am I still taking you to the Valentine Ball after upsetting you the other night?' he asked the morning before the event.

'If you still want to,' she said evenly, 'I have every intention of going, so it's up to you what you do.'

'What time shall I call for you?' he asked, as if there was nothing further to discuss.

'About half past eight. I'll be taking Marcus across to Jenna's house as soon as he's asleep, so I should be ready by then.'

'Do you want me to carry him across for you?'

'No, I can manage, I usually do.'

'Fine,' he said levelly, as if the comment hadn't registered. 'So eight-thirty it is. I'm looking forward to it. Are you?'

'Yes, I suppose so.' she said, aware that a truthful reply would be more along the lines of *I was, but now I'm not so sure.*

* * *

When he knocked on her door at exactly half past eight, Harry took a step back when she opened it to him. The dress that had graced a few cocktail parties in its time was of apricot silk and fitted her like a glove.

She'd taken her hair up and piled it in shining brown braids, revealing the slender stem of her neck and the smooth lines of her shoulders. She would be the most beautiful woman there, he thought achingly.

He wasn't the only one to be taken aback. As she took in the vision he presented in the doorway, Phoebe thought that some men looked good in a dinner jacket and black tie, some average, and the appearance of a few was heart-stopping. The man observing her with a cool hazel gaze was one of those and she couldn't believe that he had come to take her to the ball.

'I thought you had nothing to wear,' he teased as she stepped over the threshold and closed the door behind her. 'The dress is amazing and so are you.'

'It belongs to another age, a time that I don't want to be reminded of,' she replied. 'A time of wine and poses.'

'I'm not with you,' Harry said over his shoulder as he preceded her down the stairs.

'It means wining, dining, pretending—things that to some are as natural as breathing, but not me. When the chance came I got out of it, gave birth to my son in a place where he was well away from all of that and safe from psuedos. I'm happy in this new life I've chosen in Bluebell Cove, and hope that you will be too.'

He was holding out his hand to help her down the last step and when they were both on the same level he said, 'I'm working on it. For instance, it is ages since I've been anywhere socially.'

He would have preferred them to have stayed upstairs in her apartment, to give him the chance to hear anything further that Phoebe might want to tell him about her life before Bluebell Cove. But, as he'd just said, it was a social occasion, and *he* wasn't ready to tell her about *his* past, which might be what she would expect in return.

Still holding her hand, he said, 'So let's go, Phoebe. Let's head for Wheatlands Farm and the Valentine Ball.' She nodded and lifted the hem of her dress so that she wouldn't trip over it in the dark, and, with the high heels of her strappy gold sandals clicking on the hard surface of the practice forecourt, they walked hand in hand to where Harry's car was parked.

When they arrived at the farm, Pamela Enderby and her husband were waiting to welcome the partygoers in the spacious panelled hallway of the farmhouse. As they approached, they saw that she had a bouquet of beautiful flowers laid across her knee and Ian was holding a magnum of champagne.

When they stopped in front of them, Pamela presented Phoebe with the flowers and said, 'These are to say thank you for helping to save my life, Phoebe.'

'And our deepest gratitude to you, Harry,' Ian said, passing over the champagne. 'If it hadn't been for the two of you, Pamela might not have been here tonight. We shall always remember what you did for her.'

'We were only doing what we are employed to do,

Ian,' Harry said. 'So much of helping patients is being there at the right time, but thanks for your kind words...' he smiled in Phoebe's direction '...and for the champagne and the flowers.

'My aunt and uncle are here,' Harry said when they'd left the Enderbys greeting the next lot of guests. 'Do you mind if we have a word with them before we start enjoying ourselves?'

'No, not at all,' she told him, hoping that the stories she'd heard about battle-axe Barbara Balfour, as she'd been called in years past when she'd been in charge of the practice, weren't true. Her patients had been her life and the hospital had always jumped to her tune when she had been on the line or visited it in person.

She recalled how Francine, the French wife of Ethan Lomax, had come under her scrutiny, even though Barbara no longer had any say in the running of the practice. When the man that she'd loved like a son had been stressed and very unhappy, it had been Barbara who had brought Harry home from Australia to save Ethan's marriage.

Barbara was normally to be found in a wheelchair due to advanced rheumatoid arthritis, and tonight was no different when the two of them presented themselves to her.

At a first glance Phoebe took an immediate liking to Barbara's husband, but observed Harry's Aunt Barbara warily as she asked him, 'So who is this that you have brought to meet us, Harry?'

He smiled. The days were long gone when Aunt Barbara ruled the roost. 'Phoebe is the district nurse

I told you about, who is based at the surgery,' he explained.

'Ah!' she said, and he thought she had only to hear someone refer to the practice and she was tuned in.

'And so where do you live?' she asked, and listened with raised brows as Phoebe told her, 'I live in the opposite apartment to Harry.'

'And do you have family?' was the next question.

'I have a child, yes.'

'Are you married?'

'No. I'm divorced.'

Phoebe would have been annoyed at the woman's impertinence if it hadn't been for Harry's desperate expression. He was listening tight-lipped, eyes rolling heavenwards, and taking her arm, was ready to move on to the dance floor with a brief goodbye to his relations.

'I'm so sorry about that,' he said as he took her in his arms. 'I'd forgotten just how much my aunt thinks she owns Bluebell Cove.'

'Don't be,' she said. 'She is only looking after your interests, protecting you from the husband-hunting part of the local community—clearly she thinks I might be one of them!'

'And are you?' he asked quizzically, with his good humour restored.

'That's for me to know and you to find out,' she said laughingly, and with the heady excitement of being dressed up and out for the evening with the man that she so easily could fall in love with making her heart beat faster, she gave herself up to the moment.

There was a buffet in the interval decorated with red

hearts and ribbons and a red rose for every lady present. As they were about to eat, Ian Enderby said he had an announcement to make.

When they heard what it was there was much cheering and laughter among those assembled there. It seemed that a young man at the ball had taken the opportunity on such an appropriate occasion to propose to his girlfriend, and she'd accepted. Soon waiters were bringing round glasses of champagne, courtesy of their host, for those present to drink a toast to them.

Phoebe was smiling as she raised her glass, but Harry's expression was sombre and she wondered what was in his mind.

The rest of the evening passed pleasantly enough. They spent some time chatting to Maria, the youngest of the practice nurses, and her boyfriend, and shared a table with Jenna, and her husband Lucas, who was clearly head over heels in love with his bubbly blonde wife. But Phoebe couldn't help feeling that the magic had gone ever since they'd toasted the St Valentine's Day lovers.

'What's wrong?' she asked, as Harry drove them home in the dark night. 'You were enjoying yourself until we drank the toast to the young couple.'

He nodded. 'Yes, I know. I'm sorry for being such poor company. It just hit me that they were so sure, so ready to commit to each other, with no idea of what fate might have in store for them.

'That was how it was with my parents—fate had something dreadful in store for them that they never came to terms with, and I suffered greatly as a result.

'We were all happy and content until they lost my baby brother to a serious illness, and after that I was left out in the cold while they grieved for him evermore.

'So you can see why I'm wary of playing at happy families. I would never do that to a child of mine, and one way of making sure is to stay clear of that kind of thing,' he concluded flatly, gazing straight ahead with his hands tight on the steering-wheel.

'You are wrong to think like that,' she said gravely. 'You would make a wonderful father if you would put those sorts of thoughts out of your mind. Don't let your parents' inability to cope with their grief blight *your* life, Harry.'

He gave a dry laugh. 'Thanks for the vote of confidence, but I'm not ready for playing mothers and fathers yet.'

The practice building was in sight. It was time to pick Marcus up from Jenna's house, hopefully still sleeping, but she didn't want to leave Harry in this sombre frame of mind. Her spirits lifted when he said, 'Let me carry him across this time, Phoebe.'

Was there hope that Harry might change his mind one day because of the protective affection he was beginning to feel for Marcus?

CHAPTER SIX

MARCUS was still asleep as Harry picked him up and cradled him in his arms. Phoebe wrapped him in a blanket while Lucy looked on approvingly and said, 'I haven't heard a sound out of your little one, but Lily has made up for him! She's been the one exercising her lungs tonight.

'Jenna has just phoned to say that they're on their way and then Lucas will take me home. So, how was the ball? Was it up to the usual standard of a combined Enderby and events committee occasion?'

'It was wonderful,' Phoebe told her with her glance on Harry, who didn't respond, and she thought it was incredible that they had disrupted the foundations of each other's lives with their totally different viewpoints.

When Marcus had been tucked up in his own cot once again, Phoebe plucked up her courage to reach out to the clearly still-hurting Harry in the only way she could think of. Taking a deep breath, she said, 'You shouldn't be on your own tonight, Harry, not after that painful reminder of the past. Stay here with me.'

He'd been about to depart, but stopped and asked, 'In what capacity?'

She met his gaze steadily, for once not trying to hide the feelings for him that shone in her eyes. 'Whatever you want it to be.'

Harry dragged in a swift breath then exhaled slowly. 'No, thanks just the same, Phoebe.' He gave her a self-deprecating smile that took the sting out of his gentle rejection. 'I'll be fine if you'll just forgive me for ruining your evening.'

'You didn't. So don't concern yourself about that,' she replied. But she couldn't let him walk out of her door without trying to express her affection and support for him. As he turned to go a second time she caught his arm and pulled him round to face her, cupping his face between her hands. As his arms went around her, she was reminded of the gentle way he held her son, and his heart-breaking childhood loss of his baby brother. She said softly, 'You like holding Marcus, don't you?'

He was smiling. 'Oh, so you've noticed? How could I not? He is delightful, and do you know what, Phoebe? I like holding you too.' Bending, he planted a butterfly kiss on her lips and then with the smile still there said, 'I'm going before I give in to temptation and accept your offer to stay the night.' Closing the door quietly behind him so as not to disturb the sleeping child, he went.

In the silence that followed Phoebe decided that after their bleak conversation in the car on the way home she understood him better, and would expect nothing from him until he was ready to let the past go.

If that never happened, at least she would have known him, admired and respected him, and above all else loved him for being the man he was.

* * *

After the highs and lows of Friday night, the weekend felt like a non-event. Harry didn't appear, though she imagined he was there behind the old oak door. So keeping to her usual routine Phoebe did some chores, put the washer on, and in the early afternoon of Sunday took Marcus out in his baby buggy for some fresh air.

The days were lengthening. The next event in the village would be Easter and she'd heard rumours of an Easter Bonnet Parade, which sounded interesting. But spring had yet to wrap itself around Bluebell Cove, when it did the whole village would come alive. There would be families down on the beach, the cafés and restaurants would raise their shutters, and the farmers would rejoice to see another winter gone. Already there were newborn lambs in the fields, staying close to their mothers, and each time one came near them Marcus squealed with delight.

A turn in the path brought them to the gates of Glades Manor, which Harry had viewed some time ago. She stopped to admire the lovely old house that must have caught his imagination or else he wouldn't have gone there. Yet as far as she was aware, he had made no further ventures into the property market so might have changed his mind.

She'd seen no one on the leafy lane where the manor house stood, so turned quickly when she heard a twig snap behind her. She was taken aback to see Harry there, observing her in surprise and asking, 'So what has brought *you* here?'

'I saw the house advertised in the estate agent's

window,' she told him, improvising quickly. 'That's *my* excuse for dreaming. What's yours?'

He didn't reply. Marcus had seen him and was straining against the harness that was strapping him into the buggy and crowing with excitement. As Harry bent over him, he was struck by how much the little one had grown in the short time he'd known him. A worrying thought suddenly occurred to him. 'He's going to be walking soon, Phoebe, and the apartment above the surgery won't be a safe place for an active toddler. He'll be down the stairs to where cars are arriving on the surgery forecourt if you're not careful, or even darting into the road.'

'I'll have to acquire a gate for the top of the stairs to prevent that, won't I?' she said equably. 'The thought of Marcus being in any kind of danger is not to be contemplated. I know what you say is right, but I am doing my best for him under the circumstances, Harry. I'm sorry that you don't think it is good enough.'

'I don't think anything of the kind,' he protested. 'But the fact remains that Marcus needs to be out of that sort of situation. This would be a fantastic place for a child to grow up in. I could buy it, I suppose, and turn some of the rooms into an apartment for you and him.'

She was observing him as if she hadn't heard right. 'What do you mean?'

'I was thinking it would give him a more stable background.'

'Which is something you don't think I'm capable of,' she said slowly, stunned to discover how far apart their dreams were. Harry would be happy to have her in his life as a tenant, but not as anything more. So it was still there, the backwash from an unloved childhood. He wanted the best of both worlds—she and Marcus in his life but only on the fringe of it, not taking the risk to open his heart to them fully and consider how perfect they might be as a little family.

Bending, she released the brake of the buggy, and when he took hold of her arm in a restraining grip she shrugged it off in fury. With a look that dared him to follow her, Phoebe stalked off into the winter afternoon.

Watching her depart, he couldn't believe that she could have thought there was criticism in what he'd said, when his comments about Marcus's safety had only been prompted by genuine worry. Since meeting Phoebe, he was getting a whole new slant on care and caring. She was the best, the brightest, and coped brilliantly in an undeniably difficult situation. He'd let himself get carried away at the sudden thought of the three of them living in the manor house, but had skirted around the real issue—his deepening affection for her—by babbling on about an apartment for her and Marcus as if he didn't want them to be a real family.

It had been totally tactless, but the idea of buying Glades Manor wasn't going to go away. As he looked around him at the spacious grounds and elegant stone structure of the place, he knew that was what he was going to do. But he would ask the estate agent to keep the sale under wraps until he was ready to move in…if ever.

By the time Phoebe arrived back at the apartment,

she'd cooled down and was admitting to herself that Harry's comments had been right. Pretty soon, the apartment *would* be unsuitable for Marcus, but nothing was going to take away the bitter taste of the insultingly patronising way he'd suggested that she might want to be *his* tenant, as if living on the surgery premises was wilfully putting her precious baby's life in danger.

So much for her dream that one day he would realise what he was missing in the lonely existence he'd committed himself to, but if that was his choice, it wasn't for her to interfere.

Yet it didn't stop her from dreaming about Glades Manor and its surroundings that night, and Phoebe's first thought on waking up next morning was that, on the fringe of her life or not, Harry had been ahead of her in pointing out the dangers that would be present when Marcus became mobile.

As the days went by, she decided sombrely that she'd got avoiding Harry down to a fine art. If she heard him go down the stairs first in the morning, she kept to her usual routine, driving straight to the nursery with Marcus and staying there longer than usual, until it was almost time for the first surgery of the day. That way, she knew he would be occupied by the time she got to the practice. If she was first down the stairs, she left Marcus in the car while she sorted out her calls and then set off for Tiny Toes just as Harry appeared. Afterwards, she went straight onto the district and didn't return until the two doctors were involved with the second surgery of the day. Then it was a matter of inputting her patient reports on the computer and at four o'clock driving off to the nursery again.

Once she returned it was a matter of going straight upstairs and shutting the door behind her. As Harry made no attempt to communicate during the evenings, it seemed as if he was getting the message. If she did have any doubts about it, the sardonic gleam in his eye on the few occasions when they did come face to face was answer enough.

Easter had arrived, and with it the uplifting feeling that winter had finally gone.

There *was* to be an Easter Bonnet Parade through the village on the Monday of the holiday weekend with a prize for the best entry, followed by the traditional cream tea in the village hall.

All the female staff at the surgery had been persuaded to take part by the vicar's wife and, in the week before the event were searching around for something exciting to wear on their heads. Phoebe was among them and wishing she wasn't.

There was so little time to prepare, she thought in frustration. Her evenings were taken up with Marcus, meals and what seemed like endless chores, and since the scales had fallen from her eyes with regard to Harry it was hard to work up any enthusiasm for anything except her child.

But when she went up to her apartment in the late afternoon of the day before Good Friday, there were two carrier bags outside her door. When she investigated their contents her eyes widened.

In the smaller of the two there was a cuddly Easter bunny and a chocolate egg with his name piped across it in icing for Marcus. In the bigger bag was a similar egg with *her* name on it, and incredibly, underneath it, wrapped in folds of soft tissue, was a brightly coloured pillbox hat decorated with a plume of feathers and a dress from the same 1950s period with a nipped-in waist and swing skirt.

The card with them said:

These belonged to my mother and were among some things of hers that Aunt Barbara has kept stored for me. Would they be of any use to you for the parade?

A lump had come up into her throat at the unexpected thoughtfulness of Harry's gesture, and she cringed to think how petty her behaviour must have seemed since the episode outside Glades Manor.

At the bottom of what he'd written was a P.S. that gave some indication of *his* feelings regarding that. It said:

I'm not trying to get back into your good books, though I miss your sunny smiles. It was just a thought, Phoebe, and an opportunity for them to come out of their wrappings for once.

The surgery closed at six-thirty, but it was almost seven o'clock when she heard him coming up the stairs. When he reached the landing she flung open her door and came out to face him wearing the dress and hat.

If he hadn't already been conscious of her enticing curves, he was now as the dress fitted perfectly, and the hat, perched on top of the shining swathe of her hair, completed the picture. In a moment the stresses of his working day were wiped away by the vision she presented.

'Wow!' he breathed. 'You look fantastic! You don't do things by halves, do you?'

She was pirouetting in front of him and smiling. 'No, I don't. I just wanted to say that I would be honoured to wear your mother's lovely clothes, and thank you so much for thinking of me. There must have been some bright days in her life. Did she buy them for a special occasion?'

'I don't know,' he replied, 'but while running the stables my parents mixed with some of the wealthiest folk in Bluebell Cove. I suppose they had to be part of the social round to find their customers.'

'Yes, that would seem possible,' she agreed. 'And now that you've had a viewing, will you step inside for a moment and help me with the zip of the dress? I think that it's caught in the fabric somehow.'

'Yes, of course,' he replied, and followed her into her sitting room. As he bent to free the zip his hands brushed against the smooth skin of her back. He became still as the desire that had risen in him when he'd seen her in the dress and the hat spiralled.

When she swivelled round to face him questioningly, he gave one last pull at the zip and the dress fell to the floor, revealing silky underwear that did little to cover her gently curved figure. Phoebe could feel it again, the heat, the pull of the attraction he had for her, and she for him.

'Where's Marcus?' he asked in a low, strained voice.

'Asleep,' was the breathless answer.

'That's all right, then,' and with a thankful smile, Harry took her face between his hands and kissed her hard on the lips. Then his mouth was caressing her neck and the rise and fall of her breasts in the flimsy underwear.

'Can I take them off?' he murmured.

'Mmm. Yes, please.'

'And the hat?'

'What? Oh, yes, of course, by all means,' she said laughingly, catching a glimpse of herself in the mirror. Then everything else was forgotten—the hurt of what he'd said outside the manor house, the way he'd taken the joy from another occasion like this by calling halt at the height of their desire. For now that same passion was back again, stronger than before.

They were hungry for each other, blending as if they were one, and when their desperate longing for each other had been appeased, Phoebe lay close to his chest between the sheets of her bed and said dreamily, 'You must be starving. I'll make you something to eat.'

He kissed the tip of her nose and sighed as he explained, 'I'm expected at Four Winds House for my evening meal and can't let them down. Their lives are so restricted these days that even something as unexciting as having *me* to dine with them is an event.'

She gave him a gentle push and told him, 'Go on, then. You've just given some meaning to *my* restricted life, so now go and liven up theirs. I've never worked under that formidable woman, but can still appreciate her past worth to the community here. Yet she has got some nerve, grilling me about Marcus and my marriage! Jenna is lovely so she must take after that nice father of hers.'

'Yes, she is. It's only since Barbara had to give up the practice that she's really had any time for her husband and daughter.'

'She'll probably give all the affection that Jenna never had to little Lily.'

'Yes, maybe. Better a generation late than never, I suppose.'

He was getting dressed and she lay watching him, admiring the strong flanks, the broad chest, the arresting face. Harry was some guy, she thought. He was taking her out of the lonely world she'd been simply existing in and bringing her to life. So why did she feel that if it came to any kind of total commitment, he would hesitate?

'What are you thinking about?' he asked, tuning into her change of mood.

'I was wondering if you would ever use me to fill a gap.'

'Is that what you think? That I might take advantage of you, Phoebe?

'Use you for my own desires? You're beautiful and

brave, the kind of woman any man would want to spend the rest of his life with.'

'But not you Harry, because you know I would want commitment. Family life with all its ups and downs, joys and sorrows.'

Clutching the sheet around her she raised herself up against the pillows. 'Sometimes it feels as if you retreat into a desert sort of place that only you know about.'

He sighed. 'We've just been to heaven and back. Can't we live with that for a while?'

She could live with it for ever if she knew he felt the same as she did, she thought, but he was saying apologetically, 'I have to go Phoebe, or the old folks will be thinking I've forgotten.' He stopped in the doorway. 'I'm just going to have a peep at Marcus if that's all right.'

'Yes of course,' she told him, still huddled under the sheet. 'You don't have to ask. When I picked him up from the nursery today he said his first word. He must have heard it from the other children when their fathers have been to collect them.'

'And what was it?'

'*Daddy!* Strange, wasn't it?'

'Hmm, yes,' he agreed, and refrained from telling her that he was one step ahead. He'd been called out to the nursery that morning because one of the little ones had been taken ill, and when Marcus had seen him he'd held out his arms and that was what he'd said.

He'd kept quiet about it, partly because he knew that she had doubts about him and also because he'd already decided that Marcus might have used the word collectively rather than directing it at himself.

If Phoebe knew what had happened, she would be worried about the outcome of that incident. *Yet not now, surely, not after what had just happened. Their coming together had been like paradise on earth; there had been no desert places there.*

When he'd gone, Phoebe showered and dressed. Then, finally coming down to earth, she tried to decide whether to carry on with the painting of the sitting room or tackle a pile of ironing.

Not wanting to be messing with paint cans and having to change into the dungarees and old sun hat that she'd been wearing on the night that Harry had arrived, she chose the ironing, which was the kind of chore where one's thoughts could wander without much chance of a mishap.

It was late when she'd finished and there had been no sound of him returning, so she went to bed and slept with the pillow that his head had rested on held close in her arms.

When she awoke the next morning the first thing she saw was the pillbox hat on the dressing table and she smiled at the memory of how she'd still had it on her head when Harry had removed her underwear.

That was the first thing she *saw*. The first thing she *knew* was that Harry hadn't come back from the Balfours. She didn't know how she knew, but when she went onto the landing there was the feeling that his apartment was empty. When she looked out of the landing window, his car wasn't down below on the forecourt.

Maybe he stayed over at Four Winds House, she reasoned. If they'd been drinking he wouldn't have driven home, and to have got a taxi would have meant being without his car this morning.

But the headland wasn't that far away. If he hadn't wanted to drive, he could have walked back to the apartment in twenty minutes, so where was he?

As she was giving Marcus his breakfast the phone rang, but it wasn't the voice she wanted to hear at the other end. Leo was on the line and her mouth went dry as she listened to what he had to say.

'Harry is in hospital,' he informed her. 'He was admitted late yesterday evening after rescuing a couple of teenagers who'd been larking about down on the beach and been caught by the tide. Apparently they were being swept out to sea when he got there, and he went in after them.

'All three are being kept under observation for twenty-four hours at least,' he explained. 'As residents of Bluebell Cove ourselves, we both know that the sea is very cold and often dangerous at this time of year. They could have drowned if Harry hadn't been driving past along the tops and seen them struggling in the water down below.

'The hospital says that the lads are very subdued this morning as not only are they all suffering from exposure but Harry has a deep gash on his hand from where he was thrown against rocks as he was pulling one of them to safety.

'He's asking if you could go into his apartment and sort out some clothes for him, as at the moment all he has to wear is a hospital robe, and he'll need some decent gear to come out in when he's discharged. Apparently there's a spare key for his place in the drawer of the desk in his consulting room.' He indulged in a moment's curiosity. 'Are the two of you an item?'

'No,' she told him, 'but we are very near neighbours, couldn't possibly live any closer. Of course I'll sort out some clothes for him. I can take them over as soon as I've dropped Marcus off at the nursery if I can be spared for an hour or so.'

'Yes, that would be fine,' he said. 'I won't have the chance to go myself with two surgeries to cope with on my own. Without him the surgery staff will all need to pull out the stops so, yes Phoebe, do that. Have you many calls booked for today?'

'Don't worry. Nothing urgent.' She was trying to sound unfazed but inside she was horrified. While she'd been blissfully cuddling his pillow Harry could have drowned, and the thought of life without him was not bearable.

When she arrived back from the nursery, Phoebe went to find the key that he'd mentioned and once she'd found it went up the stairs to find him something to wear, as he'd requested.

As the door swung back on its hinges, it felt strange to be going into Harry's apartment with him not there. It was tidy, nothing out of place, and as she looked around her she saw that there was just one photograph of the woman he'd been married to, which was odd. A smiling blonde with sun-bleached hair and tanned skin.

Yet when she thought about it there was only the odd snapshot of Darren and herself in her place, so maybe it wasn't that strange. But she was not someone to pry and, opening his wardrobe, picked out a change of clothing for him.

As she locked the door behind her she wondered if Harry had ever done anything about his interest in Glades Manor. She shuddered to think that if the fates had been less kind last night on the seashore, he might never have had the chance to buy the place, even if he'd wanted to.

She found him in a small side ward when she arrived at the hospital gazing morosely into space, but his expression changed to relief when he saw her and his first words were, 'Am I glad to see you, Phoebe! Have you brought me some clothes?'

Nodding she went to sit beside him and took his hand in hers. 'I hope you'll approve of what I've chosen.'

'I don't care what you've brought as long as they cover me up and I can get back to the surgery.'

'Leo said they were keeping you in here for twenty-four hours.'

'I've persuaded them to discharge me as soon as I have something to wear.'

She looked down at his left arm, which was heavily bandaged, and asked, 'So what's the damage to your arm?'

'Severed tendon. They operated on it not long after I arrived.'

'In that case, you do need to stay in a bit longer. I'm amazed that you've talked the doctors into letting you leave! Surely that's quite irresponsible?'

'No more irresponsible than what I did earlier in the evening,' Harry muttered under his breath. Phoebe's suggestion that he might just be using her was crystal clear in his memory, and to his shame it wasn't entirely undeserved.

Shock had her sitting up straighter. 'Meaning?'

Harry took a deep breath and tried to explain his conflicted emotions. 'Making love to you when I don't know my own mind half the time perhaps isn't the most sensible thing to have done.'

Phoebe was horrified at his words. 'Well, any pleasant thoughts I might have regarding it in the future will be soured by what you've just said! We were both consenting adults.' Her voice broke. 'I slept with the pillow you'd had your head on cradled in my arms. I was frantic when I realised that you weren't there when I knocked on your door this morning.'

He was observing her sombrely, thinking that he'd been blessed from the moment of meeting this wonderful woman, so what was the matter with him, why didn't he tell her so? But the scars of his emotionally bleak childhood ran too deep to allow the words to form. If anything, the heavenly experience they'd shared in each others' arms yesterday had made him realise how little he had to offer her.

She deserved someone who could truly appreciate her warmth and caring nature, and he knew he wasn't that man for her or good father material for Marcus.

He was going to have to find the courage to pull away from them soon—it was the only fair thing to do. But right now it seemed too cruel, especially as he was so touched by her evident concern on his behalf.

Instead, he said flatly, 'I stayed very late at Barbara and Keith's. She was unwell and I wasn't prepared to leave her until she felt better. There was a full moon when I was driving home and that was why I saw what was happening down below on the beach.'

'You don't have to explain yourself to me about anything,' she said grandly, getting to her feet.

She picked up the holdall that his clothes were in. 'I'm taking these back until tonight. It is too soon for you to be leaving after being operated on such a short time ago and I'm sure the doctors will agree with me when I tell them there is a change of plan. I'll see you this evening.'

'What about Marcus?' he said as she was leaving the ward.

'What about him? I'll bring him with me, or ask Lucy to mind him. We managed all right before you came on the scene, you know, and will continue to do so now. And here's another little item of news to cheer you up—the nurse at the desk in the big ward said that the press are coming to see you. If you can't manage a smile for me, perhaps you'll be able to dredge up one for them.' With that, she swept out of his room, leaving him gaping at her cutting farewell, and went to find the doctor in charge. He agreed with her that Harry would be better staying there for a few more hours.

'An amazing guy,' he said. 'Couldn't care less about

himself. Those kids were so lucky that it was someone like him who went to their assistance.'

By the time Phoebe reached the car park her righteous indignation was dwindling, but by no means gone. It was true what the other doctor had just said, but it was also true what *she'd* said to Harry. Though he might be attracted to her lack of suntan and smooth, pale skin, he was about to discover that she was no doormat—if he thought he could take her to heaven in his arms one day and then explain it away as a mistake the next, he had another think coming!

Everyone at the surgery was eager to know how he was when she got back in the middle of the morning and Leo asked, 'Did you take him some clothes, Phoebe?'

'Yes, but I brought them back with me,' she explained stiffly. 'He had been operated on in the early hours for a severed tendon and I didn't think he was fit to be discharged yet, although he'd already fixed it up with the doctor in charge. So I went to see him and unfixed it.'

'Harry wouldn't like that,' he said laughingly. 'But what a guy, going into the sea fully clothed to rescue not one, but two crazy kids.'

'He could have been drowned, and those lads as well,' Lucy commented from behind in sepulchral tones. Phoebe thought it was only men who could see something to rave about when distress and danger were the topic of conversation. For a woman it was always fear and dread that filled *her* mind.

Leo was the second member of his sex that she'd

spoken to who'd been impressed by what Harry had done. And to be honest, so was she, and so would a lot of the Bluebell Cove locals. But now he had to be sensible and leaving hospital only hours after an operation was not a good idea. In fact, she might hang onto his clothes until next morning and risk his frustration.

By the time she'd finished her rounds, dealt with the paperwork and picked Marcus up, she'd decided that was what she was going to do. She knew he would be furious with her, but another night under medical supervision would do him no harm.

As the evening wore on she was expecting the phone to ring any second and hear his voice asking why she hadn't kept her promise, but the line remained dead, and as the hours crept by she told herself that Harry's silence was worse than having to put up with his indignation.

She would go to the hospital first thing after she'd dropped Marcus off at the nursery, as she'd done the day before.

When she walked into the ward the next morning he was seated by the window, reading the morning paper, and when he looked up he said, 'You've just got here in time. Another five minutes and I was going to make a run for it in this flimsy dressing gown and risk being arrested at the bus stop.'

'You could have got a taxi.' she told him mildly, waiting for the storm to break.

'Yes. I know,' he said dryly, and there was a glint in the dark hazel eyes that had observed her so tenderly a couple of nights ago, 'but I didn't want to be missing when you'd taken the trouble to bring my things. Phoebe, I have to admit that you were right. I did feel rather groggy after you'd left and would have been pretty useless at the surgery if I'd gone there straight from here too soon.' He was getting to his feet. 'But I'm fine this morning so can we get moving once I'm dressed?'

'Yes, of course, that's the idea,' she told him, 'just as long as you've had some breakfast. And by the way, what about those two boys?'

'They're going home today feeling rather stupid. Both of them are local so should have known better, though I was just as crazy at their age.'

While he was getting dressed in the adjoining bathroom, Phoebe thought that he'd mentioned his childhood again, but there was never any direct reference to his parents apart from what he'd said about his mother's dress and the hat, and in the car on the night of the Valentine Ball had mentioned briefly their grief at his brother's death.

Harry knew what had happened to her father and then her mother but they'd never talked about his immediate family. His aunt and uncle, yes, his cousin Jenna, yes, but not his mother and father, not as individual people anyway.

If the opportunity came she would ask him. It might help her to understand him better.

CHAPTER SEVEN

THERE was silence in the car as Phoebe drove them back to the village. She could feel Harry's glance upon her, thoughtful and considering, but he didn't speak until they were almost there, and what he said was the last thing she wanted to hear.

'I could tell yesterday that I upset you, but there isn't much joy in being around someone like me.'

She didn't reply, just gripped the steering-wheel more tightly, and he went on to scatter her dreams even further. 'The last thing I would ever want would be to hurt you, so maybe we should cool our relationship.'

Without agreeing or disagreeing, she said, 'And how do we do that with us both working at the surgery and living on top of each other as we do?'

'If you remember, I thought of buying the manor house a short time ago but didn't proceed for various reasons.' *He wasn't going to mention that moment that he would soon be the owner.* 'Well, it's still on the market so I might have a rethink.

'Otherwise it means keeping our doors shut as much as possible when we're in the apartments. Maybe that way you won't find me so interfering. With regard to the surgery it shouldn't be too difficult as we only see each other briefly. Most of the time you're out on the district.'

Her thoughts were in chaos. Although she wasn't interested in being used, now Harry was coolly giving her the brush-off, it hurt more that she could ever have imagined. But if that was how he wanted to play it, he was welcome.

'Yes, whatever you say.' she told him with a casual shrug of the shoulders and fighting back tears. 'Fortunately Marcus hasn't known you long enough to get too attached to you.'

As he nodded in sombre agreement, Harry was thinking of the 'Daddy' episode, of the pleasure he'd gained in those few seconds when the little one had called him that.

And yet he was still going to deny himself what could be the follow-up to that *and* the love he sensed Phoebe had for him, because he wasn't sure that he was right for them, not sure that in the long term he would make them happy. And making Phoebe and Marcus unhappy was the most unthinkable emotional crime he could think of to commit.

The practice building was finally in sight, thank God. He was back on his own patch, with a gammy arm covered in bandages and a feeling that he'd just shot himself in the foot.

'I'm going upstairs to shave and have a shower,' he told her as he eased himself out of her small car. 'I'll be down as soon as I can.'

When he came down Phoebe was nowhere to be seen, but the rest of the staff were happy to see him back safe and almost sound. When he had a moment to spare he rang the estate agents to check progress.

As Phoebe climbed the stairs at the end of the day with Marcus in her arms, there was no joy in her until she arrived at the top and saw a bouquet of spring flowers outside her door.

Her first thought on seeing them was that they wouldn't be from Harry, not after that morning's dumping ceremony.

She was wrong. As she picked them up, with the heady fragrance of daffodils, narcissus and freesia all around her, the card with them read, 'These are just to say thanks for being there for me during the last two days. It was much appreciated, Harry.'

Much appreciated! she thought wearily. It was a wonder he hadn't enclosed a shopping voucher to complete the formal gesture. But he wouldn't have had time to arrange that, whereas a phone call to the florist in the village would have been enough to have the flowers delivered.

Was the man blind? She'd been there for him because she loved him, and did *not* want to be patronised for it.

With the spare key for his apartment that she was still carrying around she opened his door a fraction, placed them inside, and wrote across the card, *Thanks, but no thanks!*

* * *

As Harry came up the stairs at the end of the day he too was in low spirits, physically and mentally. Physically because his arm was hurting—it felt as if all the nerves where he'd had surgery on the damaged tendon were tied in knot—and mentally because with regard to Phoebe, it was as if he couldn't think straight.

It was as if he was punishing her for his inner hurts, the hurts that she'd had no part in. She'd had enough of her own from the little she'd told him, and it seemed that she wasn't to blame for them either. So why couldn't he just give in to the joy of being with her?

His mood took an upward curve when he reached the landing. There was no sign of the flowers he'd ordered, so she must have taken them in. When he'd placed the order he'd been promised immediate delivery, so if all had gone to plan they should have been waiting for her when she came home with Marcus.

The lifting of his spirits lasted until he opened his door and almost fell over the flowers. When he read what she'd written on the card he slumped down onto the nearest chair and stared into space.

She was the loveliest thing he'd ever seen, he thought, and he was so hurt and angry inside he was driving her away instead of making the most of what the fates had deemed him worthy of. But the trouble was, he didn't feel worthy of anything at the moment.

Hanging over him was the thought of the inquest into Cassie's death in just a few weeks' time. He would be going back to Australia for it and was not looking forward to the proceedings at all. Luckily there had been no mention of suspicious circumstances when the autopsy had taken place, and once the inquest was over he was hoping to return in a more positive frame of mind.

When she opened her door the next morning Phoebe's eyes widened at the sight of her flowers on the landing. He doesn't give up, does he? she thought. Can't bear to be in the wrong. But when she read the message on the back of the original card that said, *It was just to say thanks, nothing more*, it seemed as if that was exactly what Harry had done. He'd given up on her, and another empty day stretched ahead of her.

There was a new patient down on her list for a visit that morning and as she drove to the outskirts of the village, she had to pass Glades Manor. The 'For Sale' sign was still there, but she reasoned it would be. It had only been yesterday that Harry had said he might still be interested, and if he went ahead it would be the first time any man had bought a house to get away from her. So much for her sex appeal.

Whereas *he* had it all—the looks, the charisma, the captivating personality and, remembering what he'd done for the two drowning lads, a fearlessness and courage that was amazing. All of that added together came to the total of every woman's dream man and she'd had the nerve to think he wanted to be hers.

Hannah Trescott had been in hospital having intense treatment for gangrene in her foot. She'd been discharged the previous day with a recommended healing regime that was going to require regular after-care from a district nurse.

It would consist of changing the dressing every day, including weekends, keeping a progress report and making sure that the patient took the large doses of antibiotics required to keep the dreaded infection at bay.

When Phoebe arrived at Hannah's cottage down by the harbour she didn't have to knock. The door was ajar and when she stepped inside she found Hannah sitting with her foot raised in front of the log fire that was burning in the grate.

She was a hardy old woman who'd lived in Bluebell Cove all her life and had spent a lot of her adulthood fishing out in the bay and beyond. Until a stab in the sole of her foot from a sharp piece of driftwood had started an infection that just wouldn't go away and had ended up gangrenous.

'Come in, Nurse,' she called. 'I've just had a visit from Harry Balfour. Seems strange having him in Ethan's place, but me and Harry go back a long way. I used to take him fishing with me weekends and school holidays when he was a kid because his parents were always either moping or too busy.'

'Why was that?' Phoebe asked casually as she laid out a fresh dressing for Hannah's foot before removing the present one.

'They had stables just outside the village. Lived and breathed horses until his ma died after being thrown by one of 'em, and a couple of years later his pa followed her. Had a heart attack from the stress of trying to run the stables single-handed. Harry was at college at that time and found out that all he'd inherited from the two of 'em was a bankrupt business.'

While she'd been talking Phoebe had been gently removing the dressing and breathing a sigh of relief to find that there was no evidence of the infection when Hannah's foot was revealed.

'That seems to be healing nicely,' she said with a smile for the elderly stoic, 'but take care not to be on your foot too much and try not to knock it. Also, wear loose shoes so that there is no undue pressure on it.'

As Phoebe was packing up to go she asked, 'Did you request a visit from Dr Balfour, or was he just passing?'

'I didn't ask him to come,' was the reply. 'He came because he was keen to know all about the trouble I've been having with my foot, said he was sorry he hadn't managed to get to see me before for old times' sake, and I understood. Losing his wife over there and then taking over from Ethan here can't have been easy, and I believe he fished two kids out of the sea the other night, which sounds like him.'

'Yes, it does,' Phoebe agreed, not knowing what else to say. It was simultaneous torture and heaven discussing Harry like this.

'It's time something good happened to Harry,' Hannah went on to say, 'I was never sure about that wife of his, but I only saw her once when he brought her over to meet his aunt and uncle and Jenna.'

She sighed and unwittingly brought more gloom into Phoebe's day by saying, 'He might be one of those folk who never meet the right one.'

Or meets the right one and is too blind to see it, Phoebe thought as she left Hannah to her day with the promise to call again the next morning.

It was Easter Monday at the end of what had been an empty holiday weekend with nowhere to go and no one to go with, so Phoebe was looking forward to the Easter Bonnet Parade through the village and the socialising afterwards.

There were twelve contestants and she'd been told that she was number six. She was hoping that Harry would be there, if only to see her wearing his mother's hat and the dress that she'd worn on the evening when she'd needed help with the zip.

What had happened afterwards was locked away at the back of her mind, to be taken out and cherished then put back with haste because the hurt of the rejection that had followed was too great to dwell upon for long.

The vicar's wife had offered to look after Marcus while the parade was on so that she didn't have to worry about him when it was her turn. When she took him to the vicarage, the older woman said, 'I've asked Dr Balfour to judge the contestants. He is well liked and well known in the village. I felt that it would be a good way of showing our pleasure at having him back among us.'

Having Harry back is not *all* pleasure, not for some of us anyway, Phoebe thought as she went back to the apartment to get changed.

The morning had dawned bright and clear, to the relief of the organisers. She'd been really looking forward to

the event until she'd heard that item of news, and now
she was thinking how embarrassing that Harry should
be judging while she was wearing his mother's hat.

The only in-depth conversations they'd had since the
day she'd brought him home from the hospital had been
about surgery matters. She'd heard him coming and
going as the days went by, and a couple of times had
looked out of the window of her apartment and seen him
pulling off the surgery forecourt in the red car, and that
was all.

There was much laughter among the twelve contestants
lined up in the village square as they waited for the
parade to begin. Jenna Devereux was in modern dress
with a large brimmed hat trimmed with lots of roses.
Lucy from the surgery had found a crinoline from somewhere with a pokey bonnet to match and looked as if
she'd stepped out of the Victorian era, while Charlotte
Templeton, headmistress of the village school, had a
mortar board on her head, tied under the chin with
ribbons.

Meredith, who spent her days chained to the huge
cooking range in the kitchen of her guest house on the
coast road, was sporting a chef's hat bedecked with corn
stalks, and the rest of those competing were in pretty
outfits with suitable headgear.

Harry, in a chunky Arran sweater and jeans, was already in place on a small platform that had been erected
for the judging, and the contestants were milling around
him, waiting for the parade to commence.

When his glance locked with Phoebe's for a moment

he asked in a low voice, 'What have you done with Marcus?'

'He's with the vicar's wife,' she replied smoothly, and he nodded approvingly. What did he think she'd done with him? she thought tightly. Given him to gypsies? Left him making sandcastles on the beach or locked him in the apartment?

The village band had just struck up and the commentator, a retired milliner from the village, was about to introduce the first competitor. With a swing of the hips and a bright smile, Jenna began to walk around the flagged square to display her headwear.

Then it was Lucy in the crinoline, followed by Charlotte with the mortar board then a couple of teenage girls with saucy little numbers perched on their long blonde tresses. In what seemed like no time at all number six was being called.

As Phoebe did her tour of the square with Harry's gaze on her, she was wishing that it was the vicar's wife doing the judging and the man on the podium minding Marcus.

That way she could be her natural self. Her heartbeat wouldn't be pounding in her ears and the rest of her wilting with longing. But she was the only one aware of that and so strolled calmly past those gathered to watch.

No doubt when this event was over there would be a general exodus to the beach, Harry had been thinking while waiting for the event to start. Bluebell Cove came into its own on beautiful spring days such as this.

Phoebe had been thinking the same, that she and Marcus could go to the beach or maybe even to the woods. There, the bluebells that the village got its name from flowered everywhere in bright blue abundance, straight-stemmed and slender. Whatever she did, it would be better than sitting around the apartment, moping.

It was over and the winner had been announced. Lucy in her stiff crinoline and pokey bonnet had been chosen by the man on the platform and had gone up to receive a bouquet of Easter lilies and a ticket to a famous hat museum not far away.

Then everyone was transferring to the community hall for the cream tea that a band of helpers had prepared. While that was taking place, Phoebe went to find Marcus in the care of the vicar's wife.

She had to pass Harry to get to them, however, and he said, 'It's rather a crush in here, but this table has been reserved for me especially, so why don't you and Marcus join me? I haven't seen much of him lately.'

And whose fault is that? she almost said, but refrained in case her sarcasm made the situation worse that it already was.

As she was carrying him through the crowd to where Harry was waiting, her little one saw him and the smile on his face made her heart twist. That wasn't all, however. As they drew level Marcus held out his arms, Harry got to his feet, and to her dismay as he reached out for him the little tot said, 'Daddy.' Now she understood why it had been his first word.

Slumping down on to the nearest chair, she asked bleakly, 'Where has that come from?'

He was observing her sombrely above her son's curly

chestnut mop. 'Not from me, in case that is what you're thinking. I have no idea where Marcus has picked it up from, except that he said it the other day when Beth called me out to the nursery because a child had been taken ill.

'I arrived at the same time as some of the parents, mothers *and* fathers, and as some of the kids started shouting "Daddy" he joined in, but I didn't think it was directed at me.'

Any further discussion was prevented by the arrival of the food, brought over by a member of the events committee especially for the guest of honour and his friends.

As they enjoyed the cream tea, with Marcus biting on a scone with obvious enjoyment, Harry said casually, 'So what have you planned for the rest of the day?'

'Nothing special,' was the reply. 'We might go down to the beach or go to see the bluebells in the woods.'

'But of course!' he exclaimed. 'I'd forgotten this was bluebell time, so why don't we do both?'

'We?' she questioned, and he had no reply.

He was desperate to be with her, like a starving man for food, yet was aware that he was the one who'd set the guidelines and made the conditions. Short of telling Phoebe once again about his dread of the responsibilities and what he saw as the pitfalls of family life, he was going to have to abide by his own rules.

But he'd reckoned without *her* longing to be with *him* and, as if she hadn't questioned what he'd said, she asked, 'So where first, the woods or the beach?'

'Er...the woods, I think,' was the reply, 'then down

to the beach.' As they prepared to leave the community centre, he asked, 'Where's the baby buggy?'

'Across at the vicarage, and we'll have to go back to the apartments to pick up towels and change into our costumes.'

'Yes, okay. Let's go, then,' he said quickly, before she changed her mind.

It was quiet in the woods, with again only birdsong breaking the silence. Marcus had fallen asleep on the way and as Harry pushed the buggy with Phoebe by his side, an onlooker would never have guessed that they weren't the serene couple that they might be mistaken for, out walking among the bluebells.

Yet they'd been happy enough until a few moments ago, when Harry had said out of the blue, 'I'm going to be away from the practice for a few days at the end of the month.' As she'd observed him enquiringly, he'd explained, 'I'm going back to Australia for the inquest on Cassie's death. You can imagine just how much I'm looking forward to that, but needs be. I won't be able to settle to anything until it's over. The only thing in my life that I'm sure of at present is Bluebell Cove and the practice. Everything else is a blur.'

You could have been sure of *me*, she wanted to tell him, if you hadn't pushed me out into the cold. Instead, she asked, 'Us included?' with her glance on the sleeping child.

'Yes, I suppose so,' he replied.

There seemed no point in telling her that her face was always before him, that the memory of them making love was something he would treasure always, and that he wished that these precious moments amongst the bluebells could last for ever.

Down on the beach it was just the opposite from the peace of the woods. There was plenty of noise and laughter, with lots of people milling around either in the sea or playing on the sand. As she watched Harry making a sand castle for Marcus, Phoebe felt like weeping.

He looked up and caught her expression.

'What?' he asked, and with a quirky smile. 'Are you upset that I didn't choose you as the winner in the Easter Bonnet Parade?'

'No, of course not,' she protested. 'Winning meant far more to Lucy than it would have done to me. I thought you were very fair with regard to that.'

'But not fair in everything perhaps. Is that what you're thinking?'

'It might be,' she told him, adding as she picked Marcus up in her arms, 'We're going for a paddle.'

It was really warm for the time of year and picking up on Phoebe's need for a little space from him he spread out a towel on the sand and said, 'I'll join you shortly. I'm just going to try to catch the sun for a little while before it goes down.'

'There's no rush,' she replied. 'We'll be fine on our own.' As he closed his eyes against the glare Harry thought that was one for him again—a reminder that they'd managed very well before he'd come on the scene and no doubt would continue to do so.

It was his last thought before the effect of an

accumulation of restless nights took hold of him and he slept.

It was chilly when he awoke and the beach was almost deserted. He could see a lifeboat ploughing through the waves out at sea and thought that someone was in distress out there.

In the same second he realised that Phoebe and Marcus were nowhere to be seen and he was on his feet in an instant. The buggy was still there but it was empty.

He'd said he would join them soon and what had he done? Wasted precious time with them both by falling asleep. He was pathetic. It was the first time in weeks he'd been near either of them away from the surgery and he'd dozed off.

Maybe she'd gone home in disgust, he thought, and couldn't blame her if she had. 'Have you seen a woman with a toddler in the last hour?' he asked the few people who were hanging on to get every last ray of the sun and a few more breaths of sea air in their lungs.

'No,' was the only answer he received, and now he was thinking surely Phoebe wasn't so disenchanted with him that she *had* gone home, as he'd at first thought.

His mind was in chaos. No one seemed to have seen them and none knew better than him the joys and perils of this beach, unless it was Ronnie the lifeguard, or his cousin Jenna.

The two of them had spent hours on it during their growing years and knew all about the rip tides with their treacherous currents that could sweep the unsuspecting out to sea in a matter of seconds.

There was also the risk of being trapped in the caves or on the rocks when an incoming tide took them by surprise, as had been the situation before the two lads he'd saved had ended up in the outgoing tide.

His glimpse of the bright orange of the lifeboat a few moments ago was also adding to his unease, even though he knew that it wasn't always an emergency when it put out to sea. It could be on a training run for the benefit of new crew members or on a trial run after repairs.

He flung the towels into the buggy and as his glance raked over the rock-strewn beach again, he finally saw Phoebe coming slowly towards him, silhouetted against the last rays of the setting sun. With one hand she was supporting a small figure as he took wobbly steps beside her and with the other she was holding a beach ball.

Thank God! he thought as he ran towards them. 'Where on earth have you been?' he cried when he drew level. 'You've been gone ages. I was getting so worried about you!'

'We came looking for you when you didn't come to join us,' she protested, taken aback by his greeting. 'Didn't you notice that I'd covered you with the dry towels? It was getting chilly and you were so soundly asleep it seemed a shame to disturb you.

'Then Marcus saw some children with a beach ball and wanted it, so I took him to buy his own from the shop on the road above. As he is getting more keen to be on his feet every day it was slow progress. I'm sorry to have caused you anxiety once again on our behalf, Harry, but remember we are not your responsibility!'

Feeling that he'd just made a fool of himself, he

said grittily, 'If I had known that Marcus was walking by hanging onto you, I wouldn't have been thrown by seeing the buggy still here. That was why it never occurred to me that you might have gone up to the top. So maybe I'm the one who should be apologising.'

'Let's forget it, shall we?' she said gently, bemused again by the extent of his concern.

He didn't reply. Just lifted Marcus into the buggy, fastened the straps, and not another word passed between them as they left the beach behind and proceeded up the coast road to the surgery building.

He was insane to have let Phoebe take such a hold of his feelings, his heart, his life, Harry thought as they walked along in the spring dusk. She was kind and loving; everything about her took his breath away. If it had been Cassie who'd found him asleep in the chilly afternoon, she would have found a bucket of water from somewhere, thrown it over him and laughed as he'd shivered and spluttered beneath it. Phoebe's gentleness, covering him with towels to protect him against the cold, would have been completely foreign to her.

They were at the top of the stairs now and Phoebe couldn't stand the thought of them separating with a brooding silence between them. As their glances locked she reached out and touched his face gently, but to her dismay he recoiled, took a step back and said harshly, 'Play fair, will you, Phoebe?'

Turning his key in the lock, he flung the door back and almost in the same movement closed it behind him, knowing that if he'd let another second go by she would have been in his arms. It would have progressed from there, and she would still have wondered if he was using her.

It had been a lovely day until he'd woken up on the beach and found them gone, he thought wretchedly. After that it had gradually lost its charm, especially when she'd reminded him that she and Marcus were not his responsibility.

Not so long ago he would have agreed with that, been relieved to hear it, yet not so much now. His panic on the beach had woken him up to his true emotions concerning the Howard family. He knew now that he didn't want to be on the outside of their lives any more—he desperately wanted to take care of them and be surrounded by the warmth of their love. But first he had to get the ordeal of the inquest over, and until he had closure from that he couldn't ask Phoebe to marry him.

CHAPTER EIGHT

THAT settles it, she decided in the quietness of the apartment after Marcus was asleep. She was going to have to leave The Tides Medical Practice, look for a district nurse's position somewhere else.

Bluebell Cove was enchanting. She would have loved Marcus to grow up there like Harry and Jenna had, but she could not endure living so close to the man who had turned her life upside down. She loved him with all her heart, but he was constantly letting her know that she wasn't the woman of his dreams.

She wasn't sure where she would go, maybe somewhere up north, not too far away from Katie and Rob. Certainly not to London—that would always be first on her list of places she never wanted to see again because Darren lived there.

This village was different, she loved the place. But she loved the man in charge of the practice more, and Harry was here for life. He hadn't actually said so, but she could tell that being back in the place where he'd grown up was his only comfort after losing his wife.

Where she, Phoebe, fitted into the jigsaw of his life she didn't know. But one thing was clear: she was just a small insignificant part of it. If that was how it was going to be, it was a good enough reason for her and Marcus to move on.

She could still see him recoiling from her and telling her harshly to be fair as if she'd stepped out of line and he objected to the familiarity.

Put it out of your mind, she told herself firmly. Go to bed, get a good night's sleep so that you are bright-eyed and on the ball at the surgery in the morning, and at the first opportunity start job hunting.

It had sounded very positive put like that, but the moment her head touched the pillow the tears came and wouldn't stop.

Yet the next morning the determination was still with her until a wave of nausea had her dashing to the bathroom in the middle of giving Marcus his breakfast. When the retching had subsided Phoebe walked slowly to where she kept a calendar on the wall and her heart began to thump in her chest.

Her period was late. It should have been three weeks ago. How could she not have picked up on that? she thought frantically. Yet the answer was simple.

There had never been the necessity to check on monthly cycles since she'd had Marcus. She'd never slept with any other man since she'd left Darren. Hadn't had the time, the inclination or the opportunity until Harry had come into her life. Ever since their untimely meeting on the landing on the night of his arrival in Bluebell Cove, she'd been living in a different world where she'd fallen in love with a real man.

A man of honour and integrity, who was growing to

love her son and had seemed to feel the same way about her. But there was a lot of hurt inside him and he clearly didn't trust her not to make it worse, so what did she do now?

Marcus was objecting to having his breakfast interrupted by banging his spoon on his plate and switching her thoughts back to the present she made sure he was fed, then, still in a daze, prepared to face the day ahead.

In the late morning she bought a pregnancy testing kit. Returning quickly to the apartment in her lunchbreak, she used it and it was positive. She was going to have another child.

Panic was gripping her. *Harry had to know, but when?* Last night she'd had every intention of leaving Bluebell Cove but what now? Surely he wouldn't leave her to cope alone, but would he offer marriage? Of one thing she was sure—despite her love for him, she wasn't going to marry him just for the child's sake, so where did that leave her?

By the end of the day her mind was clear of the debris of confused thinking. She was still going to move on. She simply couldn't bear his hot and cold treatment of her, it was too painful given how deeply she cared for him. When she was settled, she would tell him she was pregnant and hopefully they would be able to come to some amicable arrangement.

Amicable, she thought miserably. Not joyful, tender or loving, just *amicable*.

Situations she would never agree to were a marriage, or a liaison of convenience, or him having sole custody of their child, and with those sombre thoughts in mind she resumed the duties of the day.

Phoebe was avoiding him, Harry thought as he climbed the stairs at half past six that evening, and could he blame her? He'd seen her three times during the day and on each occasion they hadn't exchanged more than a couple of words.

She'd been home in the lunch-hour, which wasn't usual. He'd seen her whizzing up the stairs as if she hadn't a moment to spare and had intended following her to apologise for the way he'd acted when they'd arrived back from the beach, but he'd been thwarted by Leo wanting a word in private and by the time he'd been free, she'd gone.

It had been the same situation in the afternoon. When she'd returned to the practice to update her patient records, he'd just started afternoon surgery. But now he was free and as he knocked on her door wished he knew what he was going to say to heal the breach between them. She must be weary of his changing moods

When he'd left her the night before, after bellowing at her when she'd touched him, he'd stood behind his closed door and shaken his head in disbelief. All day he'd been aching to hold her close, to kiss her, make love to her, yet had kept a tight hold on his feelings. But when she'd reached out and caressed his cheek, he'd felt himself weakening, and what had he done but behave like a prudish virgin! If Phoebe hadn't already got him labelled as a head case he would be surprised. But there was no way he could have been with Phoebe and felt completely at ease, not with Cassie's inquest looming.

He hadn't told anyone how he was dreading going back to Australia for the inquest, except her. It would bring the memory of all the horror and grief of Cassie's death back again, but he was also hoping for a feeling of closure. He knew he needed that if he was going to put his doubts and uncertainties to one side and ask Phoebe to marry him and make a new life together.

There was no welcoming flinging wide of the door in answer to his knock, just a few inches with her observing him warily. It reminded him of the night of his arrival, and although they'd become much closer since then, tonight it was still just a crack that she was observing him through. He wondered grimly if they were so far apart that she was actually afraid of him.

It would seem not. She was dredging up a pale smile and asking, 'What is it, Harry? I'm just about to bath Marcus.'

'And I'm not allowed over the threshold, is that it?' he questioned dryly.

'Yes, but only because it seems the sensible thing to do,' was the reply. And because she couldn't bear to see the look on Marcus's face when he saw Harry. 'He will only get too excited if you're involved in his bath time.'

He shrugged broad shoulders inside the business suit he wore for the surgery. 'Okay. Fair enough. I just came to say sorry for being so edgy last night. It was unpardonable. Can you forgive me?'

'Yes, I can, so just forget it,' she told him. 'I know you're still traumatised by what happened to your wife.' And thought there was more trauma to come that he didn't yet know about. Would Harry feel that apologies were due on a much wider scale when he knew she was pregnant?

'Yes, I am, to a degree,' he said, 'but even so that is no excuse for my...'

'Like I said, it's bathtime,' she reminded him.

'Yes, I know that's what you said,' he agreed, accepting her obvious reluctance to talk to him. 'Goodnight Phoebe.'

'Goodnight,' she said tonelessly as he turned away.

The 'bathtime' that she'd been hammering home was over. Marcus's eyelids were drooping, and as she wandered restlessly around the apartment, Phoebe was desperate to talk to someone she could trust. Who better than her sister who had already been her rock once before?

'So who is this guy?' Katie croaked in surprise when she'd finished explaining.

'Harry has taken Ethan's place at the practice, and for the first time in my life I'm so in love I can't think straight,' she told her. 'He's everything I've ever wanted in a man.'

'So do you think you're going to get married, then?'

'Er...no. The attraction is mutual, but the love is all on my side. He is a widower who lost his wife in a dreadful accident in Australia and doesn't want to tread that path again.

'Obviously he will have to know that I'm pregnant and that I will expect some support from him, but wedding bells are not on the agenda. It would be for the wrong reason, however much I love him. I'm leaving Bluebell Cove and am looking for a job elsewhere, so if you hear of anything…'

'Will you have to work out your notice?'

'Yes, unless they find someone to replace me immediately.'

'So come and stay with us when you've finished there. You know we love having you, and I'm longing to see how much Marcus has grown.'

'Thanks for the offer, Katie,' she told her. 'I'll bear it in mind, and give my love to Rob.'

'My sister wants me to go and live with her and her husband up north,' she told Janet Crosbie, the middle-aged practice manager, the next morning, when Harry was ensconced with his first patient of the day. The rest of the staff had dispersed after their early morning tea, leaving just the two of them in the kitchen.

'I'm undecided what to do, but did wonder how much notice I would have to work if I took her up on the offer. I suppose it would depend on how quickly a replacement could be found, wouldn't it?'

Janet was smiling. 'Yes, it would normally,' she replied, 'but not in this instance. I know someone who is looking for a position of district nurse locally and would fit in here very nicely…my daughter!

'Bethany and her husband have just moved into the area and that was her job where they lived before. Their two young ones have been accepted into the village school and they are all eager to settle permanently in Bluebell Cove. So you could go whenever you wish, but Phoebe please don't feel as if I'm pushing you!'

'I don't,' she told her, 'but what you've just told me simplifies things, although I haven't yet decided what to do. It is very important that I don't make the wrong decision, and, Janet, please don't say anything to Harry or the rest of the staff about me leaving, will you? You'll be the first to know when I've made up my mind. Now, I suppose I should get moving or he will be thinking that no one requires my services and that would be a first!'

It would be helpful if she could leave without any fuss or palaver while Harry was in Australia, she thought as she drove towards Hannah Trescott's cottage. But how she wished it hadn't come to this!

She'd told Janet she was undecided what to do, but it wasn't strictly true. From the moment of discovering she was carrying Harry's child, she'd known she had to leave the village. When she went, she would leave him a letter explaining about her pregnancy and making it clear that there would be no denying him an active part in the life of their child, but not as the family that he had no taste for.

For the next two weeks she was going to keep a low profile where he was concerned, making sure he didn't pick up on her condition or get too close so that all her resolve flew out of the window by just being near him.

Then it would be a case of facing up to the future as a single mother with two children.

She *was* going to accept Katie's invitation to stay with her and Rob, but only until she'd found a job and a place to live, and that was as far as she could think for now.

There was no knock on the door that evening. Harry had gone to dine with the Balfours at the close of the surgery, and if he hadn't already arranged to do that, the tepid reception he'd received the night before would have made him think twice.

Yet he had actually managed to have a conversation with Phoebe in the late afternoon, though it *was* work related. She'd sought him out to tell him that she was almost sure she'd seen a young boy with rickets while on her rounds.

'Rickets!' he'd exclaimed. 'It's an illness from a bygone age, or at least it used to be. But I do remember seeing a piece in one of the medical journals about it becoming prevalent among youngsters who spend hours in front of the television in one position. Due to their obsession with it, they don't get enough fresh air and sunlight.'

'It's a vitamin D deficiency, isn't it?' she'd said.

'Yes, basically caused by a lack of it in the foods they eat, plus not enough sun and too little exercise. So where did you come across this child? It wasn't him that you'd gone to visit, was it?'

'No. I'd gone to see his grandmother. She has a regular injection every month and is too old and frail to get to the surgery for it.'

'So who is it that we're discussing?'

'The child is Oscar, Jasmine Jackson's eldest.'

He groaned. 'Oh, no, not one of Jasmine's brood. I remember her well from before I went away. How many little Jacksons do we have now?'

'Six. Three girls, three boys.'

'Did you mention rickets to her?

'Yes.'

'And?'

'She said she'd heard that you were back and maybe you'd call round to see Oscar and have a chat about old times. Does she have a husband?'

'Yes, he's a farmhand with fists like sledgehammers,' he said laughingly. 'If she wants to see me, she can bring her child to the surgery and I'll want witnesses present, but what made you think of rickets when you saw the youngster?'

'There was bowing of the legs and enlarged wrists and ankles. Whenever I go to give the old lady her injection Oscar is always huddled in a chair, watching television.'

'Yes, but surely he's of school age. Why is he not there? Don't tell me that Jasmine lets him play truant.'

'I don't know about that, you would have to ask her, but it is my last call of the day when I see him, so he might have already been to school. From what I can see, all Jasmine's children watch TV quite a lot but, then, so do most children. Oscar is the only one showing signs of rickets, though.'

'Yes, well, we'll have a look at young Oscar and see what is going on. Ask one of the receptionists to give

Jasmine a call and make an appointment for her to bring the boy to see me, will you, Phoebe?'

'Yes,' she said, her mind elsewhere.

He was observing her thoughtfully. 'You're miles away. What's wrong?'

As if he didn't know, she thought. *Everything was wrong,* and what on earth had possessed her to ask if the woman they'd been discussing had a husband?

He was waiting for an answer so she gave him one, but again she was avoiding the truth. 'Nothing is wrong. I'm fine,' she told him, and made a speedy exit from his consulting room before he found any more awkward questions to confront her with.

When she'd gone, Harry's thoughts switched to the coming ordeal. He would be flying out to Australia in ten days' time and returning one week later. As well as the inquest, there were a few loose ends that he needed to tie up while he was there.

Yet he didn't like the idea of Leo being the only doctor at the practice while he was away, but the other man was emphatic that they would be able to manage without him for that short space of time.

Leo had spoken to him the other day regarding his apartment if he moved to Glades Manor. 'I've been very comfortable at Meredith's guest house,' he'd said, 'but I'm ready to move into something more permanent when the opportunity arises.'

'Who told you I'm thinking of buying the place?' he'd asked, and the fair-haired six-footer who always seemed to hit the right note with the opposite sex—which was more than he could say for himself these days!—had explained that Lucy had seen the estate agent showing him round when she'd been out walking her dog.

'I see,' he'd said. 'I wondered if it was Phoebe who had told you as she knows about my interest in Glades Manor. She once came across me up there while she was pushing Marcus out in his buggy, yet I can't imagine her being into surgery gossip.'

'She isn't,' Leo had assured him. 'Phoebe is a very private person; we don't see that much of her here. She no sooner appears than she's gone.'

Tell me about it, he'd thought groaning inwardly, I'm to blame for that. As he had patients waiting, he'd told Leo, 'If I buy the manor house, you can have my apartment with pleasure. I would expect that it's the only one of the two likely to become vacant. I'll make sure that Janet, as practice manager, gives you first choice, but nothing has been settled about Glades Manor as yet.'

He was in the process of buying the property but hadn't yet exchanged contracts on it. That would happen around the time he got back from Australia and it would have been a marvellous moment if Phoebe and Marcus had still been part of his life. But he knew who was to blame for that, and it wasn't them.

After the way he'd treated her he was going to be rattling around the place with his dreams shattered. He'd imagined Marcus playing in the gardens and the fields around it, sleeping safe and sound in one of the sun-washed bedrooms, with Phoebe close beside *him* when he went to sleep, and there when he awoke in what would have no longer been his lonely bed. But all of that would have meant commitment, relying on others and them relying on him. He'd given Phoebe reason to believe he wasn't able to offer that, and had been paying the emotional price ever since.

Jasmine and young Oscar came to see him the following morning after Phoebe had roused his interest in a possible rickets situation. When he'd examined the boy, his expression was grave. 'Nurse Howard was right, Jasmine,' he said. 'Your boy lacks vitamin D, which can affect healthy growth in a child.

'He's got rickets. I'm going to send him for X-rays to confirm my findings, and in the meantime increase his intake of the vitamin, make sure he has plenty of oily fish and foods that contain animal fats in his diet. Also see to it that he gets out in the sun more as sunshine can help his intake of vitamin D, and for goodness' sake limit his television watching! He should be getting exercise at his age, out kicking a ball around.'

'All right!' she cried. '*You* want to try coping with six of them on a farmhand's wage and with only twenty-four hours in a day.'

'What I'm suggesting is for Oscar's own good,' he told her. 'Sunlight and exercise cost nothing, and if you give all the family the same food it shouldn't cost any more. Also I'm going to give you a vitamin D supplement for him to take.'

She sighed. 'I suppose you're right.'

'I *am* right. I'm a doctor, Jasmine, and what your son has got was almost unheard of until recently. It belonged to past generations living in hard times. With regard to the X-rays, you should receive an appointment in the next few days and once the results have come through I'll want to see Oscar again.'

'Yes, okay,' she replied, and paused in the doorway. 'You were fun in the old days, Harry. Who's taken the joy out of you?'

He didn't reply, just rolled his eyes heavenwards and called in his next patient. Yet what the sassy Jasmine had said had gone home. If Phoebe was going to continue keeping him on the fringes of her life, joyless was how he was going to stay.

Jasmine's visit had one redeeming feature: it provided him with a reason to talk to Phoebe again when she came back at four o'clock. As soon as she appeared, he called her into his consulting room.

'I've had young Oscar and his mother here,' he said when she'd closed the door behind her. 'And you weren't wrong about the rickets. I'm sending him for X-rays, of course, but have no doubt in my mind about what the results will be.

'She was angry at the inference of neglect on her part, and wanted to know how I would like six kids to look after. I refrained from telling her that I would need a lot of practice. When she'd gone, after telling me what a joyless creature I have become, it crossed my mind that you might want to second her on that.'

'So that's what this is about, is it? Why you've brought me in here,' she said wearily as exhaustion washed over her. 'To find out what is going on in *my* mind? I'm wondering what you think gives you the right to ask. Now, if you'll excuse me, I have to pick Marcus up or Beth will think I've got lost.'

He was observing her pallor. She was white, gaunt almost, with dark shadows beneath her eyes. The pale perfection of her skin that had been the first thing he'd noticed about her was submerged beneath weariness and he said, 'I've just one patient to see. If you can hang on for a few moments longer, *I'll* go and get him.'

'No, thanks just the same,' she told him. 'Marcus is my responsibility.'

'You are still punishing me for pushing you away, aren't you?'

'Yes, if that is what you choose to think,' was her parting shot as she went to collect her child. It had been on the tip of her tongue to tell Harry that when it came to punishment she knew what it was all about. She was giving up her job, a life in this idyllic village, and about to take on twice as much responsibility as she had now, all because he wasn't ready to open his heart to love and family, and *that* was hard enough to cope with on its own.

In a sick sort of way, she was counting the days to him going to Australia so that she could depart, quietly and without fuss, for the next stage of her existence.

She rang Katie when Marcus was asleep to let her know what she was planning to do and explained that she was going to accept the invitation to stay with them until she'd found a job and a place of her own, and then she would move on.

'I can't imagine how you are feeling about all this,' her sister said, 'but whether this guy loves you or not, don't you think you should tell him now that you're having his baby? Every day that goes by without him knowing will make it more hurtful for him when he does find out. If he's already beginning to bond with Marcus, as you say, he might be over the moon when he hears about this one.'

'Yes, I know,' she protested, 'but there is one thing you're forgetting—he isn't in love with me. I thought he was but he isn't, and would only be interested in taking me on as part of the package for the baby's sake. I am not prepared to let that happen.

'I'll be leaving Bluebell Cove in ten days' time, the day after Harry has gone to Australia for the inquest into his wife's death. The move shouldn't be too hectic as the apartment is kept fully furnished by the practice. It will just be a matter of packing clothes and toys belonging to Marcus, getting into the car and driving off early in the morning before the village is awake or in the evening when the light has gone.'

'And you say you're going to leave him a letter telling him about the baby?

'Yes.'

'Will it explain where you can be found?'

'No. I will tell him where I am in a few weeks' time when I feel ready to face up to it. If I see Harry too soon after I've made the break, I might lose the determination to go through with it. He only needs to touch me and I melt, but it would seem that I don't have the same effect on him. I have to keep telling myself this—I am *not* going to marry any man who doesn't love me as much as he loves my children.'

'One of them will be his as well, don't forget,' Katie reminded her.

'As if I could.' The thought was engraved on her mind in a mixture of joy and dismay. 'A friend from the London bank phoned me the other night to inform me that Darren *has* married the chairman's daughter. They are expecting their first child and he is over the moon. It's a strange world, isn't it?' And with her glance on Marcus, playing happily with his toys on the carpet beside her. 'I have no regrets. If I hadn't left Darren I would never have met Harry. Meeting him has turned my life upside down, but I won't ever forget him.

'The problem with us is that when we met, we both had hurtful pasts. But where I've coped with mine, difficult as it was, there are unhappy areas of his childhood that still haunt him. Several times he has made it clear that he wouldn't want to risk any child of his having to experience what he did.

'So how Harry is going to feel when he knows he's made me pregnant I can't imagine, but one thing is sure—we can't go on as we are. I haven't been able to convince him that all families aren't like his, neglecting the one child that they've still got because they've lost another younger one. I couldn't see you or I doing that in those circumstances, could you?'

'Definitely not,' was the immediate reply. 'We would have been even more loving and protective of the remaining child.'

But that hadn't been Harry's experience, and that was why Phoebe knew she had to leave—because he had no happy memories of family life.

CHAPTER NINE

SPRING was everywhere in Bluebell Cove as Harry prepared to fly to Australia and Phoebe made ready to move up north. Blossom was on the trees, surfers were in the sea, which was now blue instead of winter's cold grey, and on the beach families picnicked and frolicked with their children to an even greater degree as each day came and went. Every time Phoebe looked around her, the ache inside increased.

She hadn't done anything about antenatal care as yet, there seemed no point. Better to wait until she'd moved and could register at a clinic near where Katie and Rob lived.

Harry and herself were both counting the days to misery, she thought, him having to present himself at the inquest in Australia and her rootless and forlorn, moving on into an exile that Harry had given her no choice but to impose on herself.

Her vitality was low as her body adjusted to the demands of the pregnancy, and as she coped with her workload and looked after Marcus, her concern for Harry was always at the back of her mind, especially because of what she was planning to do. Would he be relieved to discover that she was dealing with it in her own way, accepting that family ties were not his thing? Or would he be dismayed that he'd been shelved in the process of coping with her pregnancy? She wished she knew.

Yet, even so, there was comfort to be had in small doses, such as seeing young Oscar playing on the beach on a warm spring day, doing what boys did, with the rest of his family, and Jasmine calling across for her to tell Harry that she was knitting them both a jumper as thanks for sorting out her eldest. The X-rays had shown that rickets were present in the child, but had been diagnosed early enough for natural growth to be restored.

When she'd passed the message on to Harry he'd said he hoped the garment wouldn't be pink as that was Jasmine's favourite colour. She'd replied that whatever colour it was he would have to wear it as it was a very kind thought on her part, and as they'd smiled at the prospect, it had been a brief moment of togetherness.

Another time of tranquillity between them had been on a day when she'd been driving along the coast road on her way to one of her calls and had seen his car parked at the side of the road. When she'd pulled up alongside, she'd found him gazing down at the beach below where Beth and her helpers had taken the children from the nursery for a picnic.

When she'd gone to stand beside him Harry had said, 'There's Marcus at the water's edge with one of Beth's girls holding tightly to his hand. He just needs to take that one step on his own, doesn't he? It's nearly always like that—once they've done it they're off. It's just a matter of them having the confidence to attempt it. Or being attracted to something so much that they forget about holding onto a support.'

As they'd reluctantly turned away from the scene below, Harry had said, 'You do realise that once he's taken the plunge you will need eyes in the back of your head? You will definitely require a gate of some kind at the top of those stairs back at the apartments. I'll sort that out for you if you like, either make one or buy one.

'And by the way, what about the lecture for nursing staff regarding new procedures that the NHS is giving the night after next at the hospital? All of you will be expected to attend. Have you given it any thought?'

'Yes, and that is far as I've got,' she told him. 'Lucy won't be able to babysit as she'll be attending the lecture herself, and even if she wasn't I don't want to be continually taking advantage of her good nature.'

'So why don't I keep an eye on Marcus? If you remember, I once told you I haven't got any good nature to put upon, and I'm sure you don't find that hard to believe. We could leave both our doors open and I could pop in and out all the time to check on him. It's the obvious solution to the problem.'

'Yes. I suppose it is,' she said, wishing that a much bigger problem than that had such a simple remedy and not wanting to seem too eager to accept his suggestion. 'Yet it will be too early for him to be asleep when I have to leave, though I can have him bathed and in his pyjamas ready for bed before I go.'

'Fine. It will give us the chance for a little playtime before he goes to sleep, and you a chance to be with people on your own wavelength for a change, as I never seem to be on it.'

When he'd driven off she'd felt tears pricking. In those few moments Harry had sorted out two of her problems, a babysitter and a gate, but unless Marcus decided to step out on his own before they left Bluebell Cove they might not need a gate, not for the apartment anyway.

Yet they couldn't leave it behind. It would be a labour of love where Harry was concerned, not for her but for her little boy. A reminder of how much he was drawn to him, and as she looked down at her still trim waistline, it was as if they would both be taking something with them to cherish that Harry had given them.

On the night of the lecture, and with only minutes to spare, she called across that she was ready to leave and Harry came striding out of his room and took Marcus from her.

She was looking subdued and he asked, 'What's wrong? Are you thinking you've drawn the short straw?'

'If I have, it won't be the first time,' she said, noting that Marcus was content to be left now he'd seen Harry. She wondered if it was wise to let them get any closer, yet she reasoned it would only be for a few hours and her little one would be asleep for part of the time.

'I've left his bedtime bottle ready,' she told him, and

with a long last glance at the smiling pair she went quickly down the stairs into the April night.

Phoebe isn't happy about leaving me in charge of her child, he thought wryly when she'd gone. What does she think I'm going to do? Offer him a game of poker?

'But, then, she doesn't know what I'm planning when I come back from the inquest. If she doesn't turn me down after the way I've treated her, the three of us are going have lots of fun and be very happy in a house called Glades Manor. So what do you think about that, Marcus?'

In reply his small charge said the only word in his as yet restricted vocabulary…'Daddy…' and Harry wondered chokingly how he ever could have been wary of moments like this.

When Phoebe returned, he was seated beside the cot reading a book, with Marcus sleeping contentedly. He said casually, 'So how was it?' he asked casually, raising his eyes from the page. 'That sort of thing can go on a bit.'

'It was all right,' she told him. 'Lots of information about new procedures and regulations. How was Marcus? Was he good for you?'

He smiled. 'Of course. He and I are great friends.'

If he'd expected that to bring relief to her expression he was wrong, but, then, he didn't know what she did, that his days were numbered with her and her child.

It was only a short time after him looking after Marcus, and on his last day at the surgery before setting off on his grim journey, that his comments about the safety measures that would be required when he started walking came into being.

He'd been on his way upstairs to consult a medical journal he'd been reading that had information about a new drug that might benefit a patient he'd just seen. But he wanted to know more about it before he prescribed it, and on the bottom step had found the Easter bunny that he'd bought for Marcus, which he must have dropped as Phoebe had been carrying him up at the end of the day. When he picked it up, he was smiling. It gave him an excuse to knock on her door.

When she opened it wide, he held out the toy and said, 'I've just found this on the stairs.'

Marcus was behind her, standing upright but holding onto the sofa, and the moment he heard Harry's voice and saw him framed in the doorway he forgot the need for something to cling to and took a step towards him.

On the point of saying thanks for bringing the toy up, Phoebe had her back to him and Harry said in a low voice, 'Stay still, Phoebe. Marcus has seen me and is on the move. He's right behind you—one more little step and I'll have him.'

Then Marcus wobbled past her and into the arms of the man on the landing, and as Harry carried him inside she was weeping tears of regret as she closed the door behind them.

'What?' he asked, putting Marcus back onto his feet. 'What's wrong Phoebe? Are you upset that he came to me with his first steps instead of you?'

'No, of course not,' she told him, wishing that she could do the same as Marcus and walk into his arms. 'It was such an emotional moment, that's all.'

He was smiling. 'Yes, it was, and it's happened just as I'm off to Australia. I've got the wood for the gate and am working on it, but it's not quite finished, so take care until I get back.'

She couldn't stand much more of this, she thought. She'd be gone when he came back, but would have been glad to have had the gate as a reminder of how loving Harry was with Marcus.

Instead, she told him, 'Don't worry. I won't let anything happen to him. And, Harry, I hope that your ordeal will soon be over when you get there, and you can return to this place that means so much to you.'

She watched a shadow cross his face and felt she'd said the wrong thing, but didn't know why. Unless it was because she hadn't mentioned him coming back to *her* especially, but he was the one who'd set the boundaries, not her.

'I'll remember what you've said,' he replied, 'and now I must get back to my patients.' He smiled tightly. 'I'll see you in a week's time, Phoebe.'

And that was that, she thought when he'd gone. No tender goodbyes or loving words. If she'd had any last-minute doubts about what she was planning to do, they'd disappeared.

He was crazy, Harry thought when he came up at the end of the day and cast a glance at her closed door. Why hadn't he taken Phoebe into his arms when they'd been together and explained that the hang-ups and hurts that family life had brought for him had now disappeared?

She'd wept after Marcus had walked his first steps in his direction and he'd wanted to hold her close then, but she'd passed the tears off as the emotion of the moment and the opportunity had passed.

As for their cold goodbye, he couldn't wait to tell her that his future lay with her. That she was his second chance of love and tenderness. The first one hadn't been quite what he'd hoped it would be, and since meeting her he'd realised just what he had been missing,

She already had a child so might not want any more, but he could accept Marcus as his own if she would let him and be content. But his mind was leaping ahead. It was just eight hours to him leaving for the airport and in that time he had to pack, make a meal and finish the gate for the top of the stairs.

Phoebe was standing by the window when he drove off at half past two the following morning, and when he looked up, she shrank back out of sight.

His journey would be long, hers much shorter, but they would both be travelling towards trauma, and today would be the first of the rest of her restricted life.

She intended driving up north in the evening when the surgery was closed to avoid awkward questions. During the day she would be making her usual calls to the sick and infirm.

The only people who knew she was leaving were Janet and Leo. They'd had to be told because she wouldn't be working out her notice. Janet knew because her daughter was ready and willing to step into the vacancy that it would create, and Leo had to be told so that he could make some arrangements of his own.

She'd left the letter she'd written to Harry in Janet's safekeeping and the practice manager hadn't asked any questions. Clearly she was expecting it to be a formal resignation from the practice from a courtesy point of view, because her departure had taken place during his absence.

It had been the hardest thing she'd ever had to do, writing to tell him that she'd left because she was carrying their child, and that, loving him as she did, she couldn't bear the thought of him reluctantly accepting the responsibility of a family that he didn't want. She'd explained with stark simplicity, every word a knife thrust in her heart.

I'm pregnant. And any delay in the telling is because of our closeness in the apartments and us being employed in the practice. I don't want to be involved in a scandal.

My wish is to move away from Bluebell Cove, and when our child is born, we can talk about its future. You can have as big a part in its upbringing as you want, except for one thing—this new brother or sister for Marcus will live with me. I know you'll want to talk this through, Harry, but could we please leave it until after the birth?

Hoping you will understand and not be too angry. Phoebe.

When she'd handed the letter to Janet, she'd felt sick inside, but now it was time for action. Harry had gone and her last day in Bluebell Cove was about to commence.

As she stepped out onto the landing her eyes widened. The gate was finished. Propped up against the wall opposite, it was made out of pale wood and well crafted. Attached to it was a brief note that said, 'I've been in touch with a joiner who will come and fix it in position for you, Phoebe. This is his number. Give him a call when you're ready, regards, Harry.

Little did he know that the joiner wouldn't be required, she thought as the ache inside her increased. The gate was too big to go in the boot of the car but there was a roof rack above that she could tie it to. No way was she going to leave behind Harry's gift to them.

Then it was off to the nursery for Marcus's last attendance and another wretched moment as they said goodbye to Beth and her helpers.

Her final visits to her patients followed and it was difficult not to say goodbye to *them* under the circumstances. But as her departure would not be made public for a little while, it was advisable, just as it would be with the staff at the surgery.

When she arrived at a smart semi-detached house on a busy road in Manchester, where Katie and Rob had taken up residence to be near his father in care just a short distance away, Marcus was asleep, as he had been for most of the journey.

It was almost midnight and Katie came rushing out

when she heard the car pull up outside. 'Phoebe, you look exhausted,' she said anxiously. 'You go in and I'll bring Marcus.'

She nodded and told her wearily, 'He's been bathed, fed and is in his pyjamas, so you can pop him straight into bed, Katie, if you would.'

'Yes,' she agreed. 'Rob is making hot drinks and we've got Eccles cakes for a night-time snack, so come on in.'

'What are those?' she asked with a wan smile, 'A local treat?'

'You guess right,' Rob called from the kitchen as they walked down the hallway. 'They're all curranty and puff-pastryish, and the place they're named after is just down the road.'

'Sounds lovely', she said gratefully, thankful for these two caring people who were always there for her in times of need, and wondered what Harry was doing at that moment and where he was.

The inquest was in two days' time and if he'd asked her, she would have gone with him for moral support. But there had been no such request and she'd got the message, just as she had when he'd told her to back off.

Phoebe wept long and silently that first night in Katie and Rob's house. She loved them both. They were kindness itself, but the feeling that she didn't belong anywhere was threatening her resolve to make a fresh life for herself, and it was the dawn of another spring day before she drifted off to sleep.

When she awoke, the cot that Katie had found for

Marcus was empty, and as she pulled herself up against the pillows it all came back. The long journey, the dreadful playacting of her last day among people she liked and respected, and Harry far away in a foreign land with no inkling of what awaited him on his return to the village. It was a nightmare that she would never want to repeat.

But they were safe with Katie and Rob for the time being. It would be almost a week before Harry returned to Bluebell Cove and by that time she hoped to be feeling calmer. He wouldn't know where she was and when he'd read her letter he probably wouldn't want to.

When she went downstairs Katie was giving Marcus his breakfast.

Rob had gone to work and her sister said, 'I advise complete rest for a few days, Phoebe. I'll look after Marcus. Don't even think of finding somewhere to live or looking for a job. You've got to think of your baby. Things can so easily go wrong in these early months and you don't want to lose it, do you?'

'No, I don't,' she said bleakly. 'Whatever the future holds, I would never want that to happen, so I'll follow your advice.'

'I hope this guy realises what he's missing out on,' was Katie's reply to that.

When Harry's plane touched down in Australia, he was surprised to see his lawyer among those waiting to greet arrivals from the UK. As they shook hands he asked, 'To what do I owe this honour, Jonas?'

'To me feeling that you might need some moral

support at the inquest, Harry,' was the reply. 'They can be depressing occasions, so let's go and find somewhere to eat and then I'll drive you to the hotel that I've booked you into.'

When they were seated in a restaurant on the concourse, the sun-bronzed, smart-suited lawyer, who looked more like a playboy than a lawyer, said, 'So how's it going in the UK? Have you settled back into your familiar surroundings?'

'Yes and no,' he replied. 'It's great to be home, or at least it would be if *all* my previous memories of it were good.' Harry debated with himself how much more to say then decided to open his heart—Jonas was a friend as well as his lawyer, and he desperately wanted to talk about Phoebe anyway. 'I've been dragging my feet with this wonderful woman I've fallen in love with.'

'In what way?'

'She has a child from a previous marriage, but in spite of that is very much drawn to family life, which I'm not—or haven't been, I should say. But I adore Phoebe and her little one, and I'm going to do something about it when I get back.'

'Good for you. Will I get an invite to the wedding?'

'Yes, if it materialises,' he promised, and could feel his palms getting moist and his shirt collar too tight at the thought of what he would do if Phoebe didn't want him, even though he would have deserved it.

The verdict at the inquest had been one of accidental death and Harry had breathed a sigh of relief when it had ended. He'd flown straight home afterwards, two days early due to the brevity of the proceedings, and also because he couldn't wait to get back to Bluebell Cove. Now he could go forward into the new life that he was planning, with Phoebe and Marcus to show him what real love and caring was all about.

A taxi dropped him off outside the surgery buildings in the quietness of a Sunday morning. He ran up the stairs to the apartments two at a time, noticing as he did so that the gate hadn't been fixed in place. That was strange, but not so strange that he was prepared for Leo opening the door of Phoebe's apartment dressed only in boxer shorts.

'What are *you* doing here?' he asked with ominous calm, and his second-in-command stared at him.

'I've taken over from Phoebe. She's gone to live elsewhere, so I'm renting the place with Janet's permission. You remember I asked about one of these if there was ever a vacancy? As it turned out, Phoebe decided to up sticks before you did. Come on in, I've just brewed up. Do you want a cuppa?'

'No, thanks,' he said as he tried to take in what he'd just been told.

He was to blame for Phoebe leaving the village, he thought numbly. Now that he'd got his priorities sorted out and rushed home to her, she wasn't here.

'I'm assuming that you have a forwarding address for her,' he said levelly.

'No, I haven't, as a matter of fact,' Leo replied. 'She was reluctant to tell me where she was going and I don't think she gave Janet one either. In any case our practice manager is away for the weekend. I imagine that Phoebe has gone to her sister's, but it's only a guess.'

'And do you know where her sister lives?'

'I have a rough idea. She's moved to Manchester since Phoebe came to live here. As you know, that's where I come from and she knew that. One day when we were chatting she said what part of Manchester her sister lived in, and surprisingly it was the same area where I was brought up.'

'Do you know their name?' he asked, still with that false calm on him.

''Fraid not, but what I do know is that they went to be near his father, who is in a care home just a few doors away from them. My mother was in there for a short time before my sister took her to live abroad with her. And Harry, if you don't mind, I'd like to put some clothes on now.'

'Yes, of course,' he said apologetically. 'If you'll write down the directions to get to this place, I'll be off immediately,'

'Yes, sure,' he agreed, 'though what's the rush?'

'Can't stop now—tell you later,' he said as Leo scribbled down the name and address of the nursing home. 'I don't see me being back in time for tomorrow's surgeries. Can I impose on you for one more day, Leo?'

'Yes, of course,' he said easily. 'You have no idea how many times Ethan filled in for me last year when my mother was ill and I had to keep going back to Manchester to look after her.'

* * *

It was early evening and Harry had found the road where Katie and Rob lived quite easily due to Leo's mention of the nursing home. The fact that Phoebe's car was parked outside a house a couple of doors away from it also helped.

The curtains were drawn upstairs so it would seem that Marcus was sleeping up there, but of the woman he'd come to see there was no sign. Though he was longing to talk to her, he decided to restrain himself until morning and went and booked himself into a nearby hotel for the night.

Now that he knew where she was, he was calming down. To discover Phoebe had packed up and left during his short absence had wiped every other thought from his mind. He'd intended sweeping her off her feet when she opened the door to him and asking her to marry him on the spot.

Instead, he'd been confronted by a bewildered Leo, and didn't want to contemplate what he would have done if the amiable man hadn't come up with a suggestion that had helped him to find her.

He was appalled that he could have upset her so much that she'd left Bluebell Cove without a word, *and* planned the move for a time when he wasn't around. He prayed that, come morning, she would have some answers for him, if only he could get to speak to her. His only consolation so far was that her car was still outside the house.

It was half past nine next morning when he arrived back at the road where Phoebe's sister lived. He'd parked his car down a side street with the feeling that if Phoebe saw the red sports car, she would be forewarned of his presence and might refuse to see him.

He would have been round there at first light, so desperate was he to speak to her, but this wasn't like knocking on the door of her apartment. It was her sister's home where he was going to be intruding.

As he was approaching the house, he stepped back out of sight. Someone who had to be Katie had come out of the house with Marcus in his buggy and set off in the opposite direction.

He breathed a sigh of relief. That left just Rob, Phoebe's brother-in-law, to get past, and with a bit of luck he would have gone to wherever he was employed.

The trauma of leaving Bluebell Cove and the long drive to Manchester was still there, Phoebe thought, but the rest that she'd promised Katie she would have was bringing some of her strength back, though not her sense of purpose. She felt as if she'd lost that somewhere along the way.

Her sister had taken Marcus to the park and Rob was away on business for a few days, so she had the house to herself as she came downstairs from the shower, intending to do something with her hair, which had been fastened back with a rubber band ever since she'd arrived.

She'd just had a bout of morning sickness and was feeling anything but lively when the doorbell rang, and still wearing a robe and slippers she went to answer it.

When she opened the door and saw Harry standing

there, she clutched the robe more tightly around her with one hand and held onto the door post with the other.

'Hello, Phoebe,' he said gently. 'Will you marry me?'

She shook her head. 'No.'

'Why not?' he asked with the gentleness still there.

'You know why not!' she cried as the shock waves that had hit her on seeing him began to recede. 'I've explained in the letter that I don't want you marrying me out of kindness or duty.'

'Do you think I might step inside for a moment?'

'Yes, of course.' She led him into the sitting room.

Still keeping his calm, he asked, 'And what letter might that be?'

'The one I asked Janet to give you.'

'I see. I got back from Australia yesterday morning, made the disturbing discovery that Leo was living in your apartment, and learned from him that you might have gone to your sister's. He remembered a conversation he'd had with you about where she lived, and that is how I come to be here.'

'So you don't know?' she breathed. 'You haven't asked me to marry you because of what was in the letter?'

'No, whatever it might be.' He brushed it to one side. 'I've loved you from the moment of our second meeting. If you remember, the first one on the night of my arrival in Bluebell Cove was rather odd! But, getting back to why I'm here, I've hesitated to tell you how much I love you because for a long time my unhappy childhood cast a shadow over the thought of a family of my own. It has taken you, a single mother, to show me how wrong I've been, and I want to take care of you and Marcus for the rest of my life…if you'll let me.'

'You crazy man,' she said softly. 'You made me unhappy by trying to *avoid* making me unhappy! I adore you, but I left the village because I thought you didn't want me. And there was another reason as well…'

'And what's that?' he asked gently, drawing her into his arms, complete with rubber band.

'I'm pregnant, Harry. That's why I said no when you asked me to marry you. It was what I'd been dreading— that you might offer to marry me because I'm pregnant, and for no other reason. And at the back of my mind was always my ex-husband Darren's response when I told him I was pregnant with Marcus. He wanted me to get an abortion, which is why we got divorced, and I just couldn't bear to think of what I'd do if you weren't interested in being a father. I didn't know you hadn't read my letter and that you were asking me because you really do love me.'

He had become very still, had neither moved or spoken while she'd been explaining. Easing herself out of his arms, she looked up at him questioningly.

'Say something, please,' she begged.

'How about wonderful, marvellous, you amazing woman?' he cried joyfully. 'Not only do you love me but you are going to give me children, and not just one but two, because I love Marcus as if he was my own. I'm so sorry to hear the reasons why your first marriage broke up, but reassure yourself that you've just made me the happiest man in the world! Can I propose to you again?'

'Yes, please do.'

'Will you marry me, Phoebe?'

'Yes, Harry,' she said softly. 'I would love to be your wife.'

'So can I take you back with me to where you belong?'

'Yes, but remember I have nowhere to live. Can I share your apartment?'

'Just for a short time, yes.'

'And what then?'

'We'll be moving.'

'Where to?'

'With hope in my heart, I've bought Glades Manor for us and our children, my beautiful bride-to-be. I'm signing the contract tomorrow, the sale will be finalised soon afterwards. And now can we please spend a few moments making up for lost time?'

'Yes,' she breathed, 'and just think, Harry, we have the rest of our lives to do that!'

He placed his hand gently below her waistline, where his child lay safe and snug, and when their glances locked she saw something that hadn't been there before. The tranquillity that came with contentment.

When Katie returned some time later with Marcus, the scene before her was what she'd prayed for. One glance at the man who had come for his bride was enough to tell her that Phoebe had found her heart's desire at last.

'Harry is taking us back to Bluebell Cove, Katie,'

she said. 'We're going to be married as soon as we can. Thank you so much for your kindness, and we'd love you to be my bridesmaid if you will.'

'Of course,' she said, and with a smile for the man who was going to give Phoebe the love she so much deserved, 'Rob will be so sorry to have missed meeting you, Harry.'

'We'll make up for it at the wedding, Katie,' he promised.

They were ready to leave, with Marcus strapped firmly into his car seat and Phoebe on the point of saying goodbye to Katie, but one thing was missing.

'I brought something with me and don't want to forget it,' she told Harry.

'It's in the garage.'

'Okay,' he replied. 'I'll go and get it. What is it?'

'A gate,' she said laughingly. 'Your first gift to me was a gate and I will treasure it for ever.'

CHAPTER TEN

THEY'D stopped off a couple of times on the way back for refreshment and for Marcus to have a little play. Every time Phoebe saw the two of them together, it was as if all the dreams she'd ever dreamed were coming true because Harry loved her. And in the autumn, when grain was being harvested and leaves were turning to bronze and gold, there would be another child to cherish, born of the love he had for her.

She was going to suggest to him that if it was a girl they should call her Cassie, just so his bubbly and fiery first wife would never be forgotten.

When Leo stepped out of his new accommodation the following morning, he was amazed. If he'd had any doubts about whether Harry's search for Phoebe had been successful, proof was there in the sturdy gate fitted at the top of the stairs. That explained the sound of drilling at a late hour!

They'd slept in each other's arms with the contentment of lovers reunited after a long absence, as that was what the weeks of hurt and misunderstanding had felt like to both of them. Marcus was safely tucked up on the sofa beside them and once the day was under way, they would go out to buy a cot.

When they'd made love before sleeping, there had been none of the doubts and uncertainties of before to trouble them. The way ahead was clear, the past was over, they loved each other totally, and what could be more wonderful than that?

On the way home they'd made plans for the following day in the form of a visit to the solicitor on the main street during Harry's lunch-break at the surgery. There he would sign the contracts for his purchase of Glades Manor and would request an early completion of the sale.

At the weekend they would shop for furniture and fittings to grace the elegant house where they were going to bring up their children and at the same time plan a wedding.

'There are going to be some raised eyebrows when the surgery staff find out that I'm back and living with you in your apartment,' Phoebe said the next morning as they ate their first breakfast together.

'So why don't we put up a notice announcing our forthcoming marriage and inviting them to be our guests when we've fixed a date?' Harry suggested.

On the way to the solicitor at lunchtime he said, 'Janet gave me the letter first thing and, after reading it, I love you more than ever, Phoebe.'

'It was my darkest hour when I wrote that,' she told him, 'and my brightest when I opened the door of Katie and Rob's house to find you on the doorstep.

'I'd been so sure of how I was going to plan the rest

of my life without you, yet putting it into practice felt like a knife in my heart. I was weak and wilting without you, but not any more, Harry, because you love me. I'm not just part of the package that comes with Marcus.'

'You never were,' he said softly, pulling up at the roadside. 'You were yourself, beautiful and kind, loyal and understanding, and I'm going to spend the rest of my life making you happy.' Oblivious of passers-by, he reached across and traced her lips with a gentle finger and then he kissed them.

The legal business had been completed and they were driving back to the practice when Phoebe said, 'When you mentioned Janet earlier, I intended telling you that her daughter is the new district nurse. Have you met her at all?'

'Yes, briefly, and she seemed fine. So was that part of your plan when you decided to move to Manchester, fitting Janet's daughter up with a position here?' he asked quizzically.

'Well, yes, I couldn't just pack up and go leaving the surgery short-staffed, could I? It would have made life difficult for you and that was the last thing I wanted.'

'Life would have been more than difficult without you Phoebe, it would have been hell on earth,' he told her. 'Why don't we call in at the vicarage on our way back and fix a date for the wedding?'

'How about May Day if the vicar is free?' she suggested. 'Saturday the first of May. We could erect a maypole in the garden at the house and after the wedding all dance around it with me wearing the Easter

Bonnet clothes! It will be as if your parents are there with us then, giving us their blessing.'

The church was in sight and everything else was forgotten in the need to get things moving in time for the first of May.

The vicar was able to grant their request for a wedding on that date. The solicitor had already promised a quick completion, and, unbelievably, when Barbara Balfour had phoned Ethan to tell him that Harry was marrying Phoebe, the young district nurse that he'd been so protective of while *he'd* been in charge of the surgery, he'd offered them his house in Bluebell Cove for the wedding reception and accepted Harry's invitation to be his best man. When the decision had been made to go to live in the place where Francine had been brought up they had decided to keep the house in Bluebell Cove for visiting the village whenever the urge came over them, and now it would be serving its purpose.

It also meant that the whole family would be coming over from France for the occasion, Ethan himself, Francine and their children, Kirstie and Ben.

Katie, as arranged on the day that Harry had proposed to her sister, was to be Phoebe's maid of honour, and Lucy had offered to look after Marcus on the great day, and so the arrangements proceeded.

Barbara Balfour was delighted at the prospect of seeing Ethan again and completely overwhelmed at the thought of having the two men that she loved like sons together again in Bluebell Cove.

Leo, whose love life was a flourishing but fleeting thing, was taking stock and wondering whether he was missing out on something every time he saw Harry's contentment.

And, in the midst of everything, Phoebe had been for her first antenatal appointment at a birthing centre that had recently been opened adjoining Hunter's Hill Hospital in the town and been told that her pregnancy was coming along fine.

Glades Manor became legally theirs just before the wedding and while Harry was at the practice, Phoebe supervised the delivery and arranging of the furnishings they had bought. At the same time she watched two men from the village erect a maypole with bright ribbons streaming from it in the centre of one of the lawns adjacent to the house.

When Harry saw it he said, 'You aren't really going to wear my mother's things when you dance around it, are you? You looked wonderful in them, but they are quite old-fashioned!'

'But of course—just watch me,' she teased.

'Watching you is my delight,' he told her softly as she moved into his waiting arms.

All the village had turned out for the wedding of the district nurse and their GP, and as the bells rang out over Bluebell Cove, the small church was filling up rapidly.

Harry had kept his promise to his lawyer and Jonas had just arrived straight from the airport. Ethan and his family had appeared a couple of days ago and those who knew them best thought how well and happy they all looked after their traumas of the year before. It was good to know that moving across the Channel had been the right decision for them.

On a clear May morning, Katie's husband Rob walked Phoebe down the aisle to take her place beside Harry. In a wedding dress of heavy cream brocade that was stunning in its simplicity, and with a coronet of pearls on her head, she walked sedately down the aisle, linking one arm through her brother-in-law's and in the other carrying an arrangement of bluebells and lilies of the valley.

The man of her dreams was waiting and as their glances held, it was there in his eyes how much he loved her, and how much he was looking forward to their life together. But it was down to little Marcus, sitting in the front pew on Lucy's knee, to make their day truly perfect, as he spoke his favourite new words, 'Mummy' *and* 'Daddy'!

⦿™ MILLS & BOON®

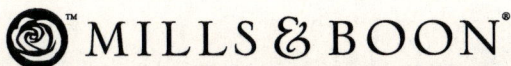

NOVEMBER 2010 HARDBACK TITLES

ROMANCE

The Dutiful Wife	Penny Jordan
His Christmas Virgin	Carole Mortimer
Public Marriage, Private Secrets	Helen Bianchin
Forbidden or For Bedding?	Julia James
The Twelve Nights of Christmas	Sarah Morgan
In Christofides' Keeping	Abby Green
The Italian's Blushing Gardener	Christina Hollis
The Socialite and the Cattle King	Lindsay Armstrong
Tabloid Affair, Secretly Pregnant!	Mira Lyn Kelly
Maharaja's Mistress	Susan Stephens
Christmas with her Boss	Marion Lennox
Firefighter's Doorstep Baby	Barbara McMahon
Daddy by Christmas	Patricia Thayer
Christmas Magic on the Mountain	Melissa McClone
A FAIRYTALE CHRISTMAS	Susan Meier & Barbara Wallace
The Soldier's Untamed Heart	Nikki Logan
Dr Zinetti's Snowkissed Bride	Sarah Morgan
The Christmas Baby Bump	Lynne Marshall

HISTORICAL

Courting Miss Vallois	Gail Whitiker
Reprobate Lord, Runaway Lady	Isabelle Goddard
The Bride Wore Scandal	Helen Dickson

MEDICAL™

Christmas in Bluebell Cove	Abigail Gordon
The Village Nurse's Happy-Ever-After	Abigail Gordon
The Most Magical Gift of All	Fiona Lowe
Christmas Miracle: A Family	Dianne Drake

1010 Gen Std LP

MILLS & BOON

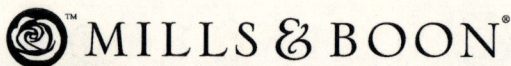

NOVEMBER 2010 LARGE PRINT TITLES

ROMANCE

A Night, A Secret...A Child	Miranda Lee
His Untamed Innocent	Sara Craven
The Greek's Pregnant Lover	Lucy Monroe
The Mélendez Forgotten Marriage	Melanie Milburne
Australia's Most Eligible Bachelor	Margaret Way
The Bridesmaid's Secret	Fiona Harper
Cinderella: Hired by the Prince	Marion Lennox
The Sheikh's Destiny	Melissa James

HISTORICAL

The Earl's Runaway Bride	Sarah Mallory
The Wayward Debutante	Sarah Elliott
The Laird's Captive Wife	Joanna Fulford

MEDICAL™

The Surgeon's Miracle	Caroline Anderson
Dr Di Angelo's Baby Bombshell	Janice Lynn
Newborn Needs a Dad	Dianne Drake
His Motherless Little Twins	Dianne Drake
Wedding Bells for the Village Nurse	Abigail Gordon
Her Long-Lost Husband	Josie Metcalfe

⊚™ MILLS & BOON®

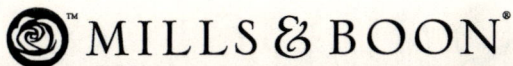

DECEMBER 2010 HARDBACK TITLES

ROMANCE

Naive Bride, Defiant Wife	Lynne Graham
Nicolo: The Powerful Sicilian	Sandra Marton
Stranded, Seduced...Pregnant	Kim Lawrence
Shock: One-Night Heir	Melanie Milburne
Innocent Virgin, Wild Surrender	Anne Mather
Her Last Night of Innocence	India Grey
Captured and Crowned	Janette Kenny
Buttoned-Up Secretary, British Boss	Susanne James
Surf, Sea and a Sexy Stranger	Heidi Rice
Wild Nights with her Wicked Boss	Nicola Marsh
Mistletoe and the Lost Stiletto	Liz Fielding
Rescued by his Christmas Angel	Cara Colter
Angel of Smoky Hollow	Barbara McMahon
Christmas at Candlebark Farm	Michelle Douglas
The Cinderella Bride	Barbara Wallace
Single Father, Surprise Prince!	Raye Morgan
A Christmas Knight	Kate Hardy
The Nurse Who Saved Christmas	Janice Lynn

HISTORICAL

Lady Arabella's Scandalous Marriage	Carole Mortimer
Dangerous Lord, Seductive Miss	Mary Brendan
Bound to the Barbarian	Carol Townend
Bought: The Penniless Lady	Deborah Hale

MEDICAL™

St Piran's: The Wedding of The Year	Caroline Anderson
St Piran's: Rescuing Pregnant Cinderella	Carol Marinelli
The Midwife's Christmas Miracle	Jennifer Taylor
The Doctor's Society Sweetheart	Lucy Clark

⊚™ MILLS & BOON®

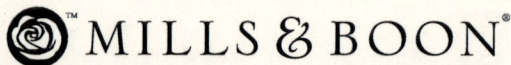

DECEMBER 2010 LARGE PRINT TITLES

ROMANCE

The Pregnancy Shock   Lynne Graham
Falco: The Dark Guardian   Sandra Marton
One Night...Nine-Month Scandal   Sarah Morgan
The Last Kolovsky Playboy   Carol Marinelli
Doorstep Twins   Rebecca Winters
The Cowboy's Adopted Daughter   Patricia Thayer
SOS: Convenient Husband Required   Liz Fielding
Winning a Groom in 10 Dates   Cara Colter

HISTORICAL

Rake Beyond Redemption   Anne O'Brien
A Thoroughly Compromised Lady   Bronwyn Scott
In the Master's Bed   Blythe Gifford
Bought: The Penniless Lady   Deborah Hale

MEDICAL™

The Midwife and the Millionaire   Fiona McArthur
From Single Mum to Lady   Judy Campbell
Knight on the Children's Ward   Carol Marinelli
Children's Doctor, Shy Nurse   Molly Evans
Hawaiian Sunset, Dream Proposal   Joanna Neil
Rescued: Mother and Baby   Anne Fraser